Dear Reader,

I am so excited to be a part of Harlequin
Flipside! I love reading—and writing!—romantic
comedy. I've discovered that it helps keep the
smile (truly, that's a smile, not a grimace) on
my face in the course of my day-to-day life.
And I'm sure I'm not alone. We all work too
hard and too much, so a good dose of humor
is absolutely necessary. It helps us keep our
perspective and maintain our attitude in the
face of, well, all of it! How else would we be
able to convince ourselves that high heels
and thong underwear are comfortable? Really,
they are! What are we thinking?

In the midst of one of those daily internal
discussions about the comfort of my clothes,
I started thinking about the price of beauty,
about our busy lives…and Anna, the heroine
of this story, was born. Her job takes all of her
attention until, suddenly, she's on sabbatical
and staring some questionable beauty regimes
in the face. Daunting for a woman who's used
to letting her hair down, eating what she wants
and not sucking in her belly.

I hope you find this story funny and entertaining.

Happy reading,

Molly O'Keefe

ROMANCE

"At no time today do I want to be naked."

Too bad Anna lost that particular battle. Finally, the spa torture was over and—bowlegged and sore in places she didn't even want to think about—she walked out the big red doors, vowing never to go back.

"Look at you, Anna," Camilla cooed. "You look wonderful."

"Let's get out of here," Anna hissed under her breath, trying to keep her clothes from rubbing up against the new hairless parts of her body.

"Anna? What's wrong?"

"I'll tell you what's wrong," she whispered furiously. "Hot wax is wrong. It's wrong in a million ways."

"I take it you didn't like—"

"Yeah, no. I didn't like."

"That's too bad because you look like a new woman."

"There is no new woman, Camilla. It's still me just chaffed." If this was the price for beauty, Anna was content to forever window-shop.

Pencil Him In

Molly O'Keefe

TORONTO • NEW YORK • LONDON
AMSTERDAM • PARIS • SYDNEY • HAMBURG
STOCKHOLM • ATHENS • TOKYO • MILAN • MADRID
PRAGUE • WARSAW • BUDAPEST • AUCKLAND

ISBN 0-373-44189-4

PENCIL HIM IN

Copyright © 2004 by Molly Fader.

This edition published by arrangement with Harlequin Books S.A.

® and TM are trademarks of the publisher. Trademarks indicated with ® are registered in the United States Patent and Trademark Office, the Canadian Trade Marks Office and in other countries.

Visit us at www.eHarlequin.com

Printed in U.S.A.

ABOUT THE AUTHOR

Molly O'Keefe grew up reading in a small farming town outside of Chicago. She went to Webster University in St. Louis where she graduated with a degree in journalism and English and met a Canadian who became her college editor and later her husband and tennis partner. She spent a year writing for regional publications and St. Louis newspapers, before she began moving around the country and writing romance novels. At age twenty-five, she sold her first book to Harlequin Duets, got married and settled down in Toronto, Canada. She and her husband share a cat and dreams of warmer climates.

Books by Molly O'Keefe

HARLEQUIN DUETS
62—TOO MANY COOKS
95—COOKING UP TROUBLE
    KISS THE COOK

For Rye and McKenzie
who have made our family a lot more fun!

1

"I'M GOING TO NEED those meeting notes by tomorrow," Anna Simmons called over her shoulder to her assistant as they made their way out of the empty boardroom.

Anna could hear Jennifer behind her, shuffling papers and...yep, cursing under her breath. Jen had a mind like a tack, organizational skills not to be believed and a mouth, at times, like a trucker. Anna kind of liked that about her.

"We'll want to send champagne to Aurora and..." Anna considered for a split second, the sound of her heels hitting the tiles echoing through the offices of Arsenal Advertising. Jen's did the same right behind her. "Some daisies." She turned left in the Creative department and headed toward the right corner of the Arsenal offices. Her corner office. Anna's lip curled for a second. "You getting this, Jen?"

"Yes," Jennifer answered, apparently not at all trying to keep the frustration out of her voice. Perhaps it was time for Anna to have a little talk with Jen about this attitude she was developing.

Anna cruised past Jennifer's desk and threw open the door to her office. She continued across the hardwood floor toward her desk. "Creative's going to need to be briefed and..." Anna paused. Jen's footsteps were no longer behind her. And the grumble had stopped. Anna turned and Jen was not there. Anna walked back to the doorway.

Jennifer was sprawled out at her desk. Head back, her long blond hair falling down the back of her chair, her arms were out, her eyes shut, she looked like she was asleep or dead.

Her very chic and painful-looking stacked heels were kicked out into the hallway.

"Jen?" Anna asked, surprised. She had never seen the classy and together Jennifer look so...undone.

"Anna?" Jen mumbled, her eyes still shut, her lips barely moving. "Have you noticed that we are the only people here?"

"It does seem quiet." Anna looked into the darkened offices with empty chairs and blank computer screens. "Where did everyone go?" she asked. There was still so much work to do. The meeting had only ended a few hours ago.

"It's seven o'clock on a Wednesday night, Anna...."

"You're right, we should order some dinner." Anna leaned against the doorframe. It was so easy to forget, in the heat of the deal, to eat. And she suddenly realized she was starving.

"No, Anna." Jen's eyes opened, her head came up off the back of her chair. "I'm leaving."

"Leaving?"

"Yes, as in going home." Jen pulled her body upright. "As in bed. And sleep. Sweet, sweet sleep." She opened a big drawer in her desk and pulled out her purse.

"But, Jen, there's still so much work to do. We have—"

"I spent the night here, Anna." Jen's brown eyes snapped and Anna took a step back. "I was here all last week until midnight."

Anna was well aware of the schedule they had been keeping. She rubbed her neck which she was beginning to think had permanent damage from sleeping on the couch in her office.

"You can fire me, Anna, but I am going home."

"Fire you?" Anna asked, shocked. "Jen, I'd never fire you." Jennifer and her hard work and fanatic attention to detail had been a huge part of the success they had achieved in the boardroom today, finalizing a deal that had been months in the making.

"I wish you would," Jennifer mumbled as she went about shutting down her computer. "Swear to God, I'd finally get some sleep."

Anna quickly realized she had worked the very hard-working Jen too hard. "Go home. Take the rest of the week off."

Jen suddenly looked at Anna as though she had grown two heads. "Really, Jen. You did an amazing job today. I could not have done this without you." Jen's mouth fell open and Anna was embarrassed. Was she such a bad boss that a little recognition was shocking?

Jennifer sat back in her seat, her brown eyes looked tired but still sharp. "It's about time you noticed that," she said. "You can fire me—"

"Jen, I am not going to fire you."

"But, I have got to say, you have the worst case of tunnel vision I have ever seen."

Anna smiled—nothing wrong with a little tunnel vision. "Well, it certainly paid off today didn't it?"

Jen grinned back, albeit a little weakly and Anna felt a serious tug of appreciation for her. "Let's go get some drinks," she said, surprising herself. "Celebration drinks." They could have those Cosmopolitans everyone loved. Anna would bet Jen loved Cosmopolitans. The two of them had never done that, gone to happy hour together after work. Well, Anna had never done that, perhaps Jennifer did.

"Drinks?" Jen asked.

"Sure." Anna nodded her head definitively. Though as soon as the words had come out of her mouth she began thinking of the amount of work she needed to do. But if Jen wanted drinks; drinks it would be.

"You...ah...you and me?" Anna read horror all over the girl's face and remembered why she never went to happy

hour. Anna wasn't the most popular person around Arsen
"Uh…"

"Never mind." Anna saved Jennifer the trouble of comi
up with some lie to avoid socializing with her. "Go hor
and I'll see you Monday."

"You should go home, Anna," Jennifer said softly.

Anna nodded, having no intention of doing that, and sh
her office door behind her. She leaned back against it. S
wasn't bothered by Jennifer not wanting to go to a bar wi
her, but Anna deserved some drinks.

After what happened in that boardroom I deserve a parade, she
thought.

She closed her eyes and for a moment just felt blank.
Empty. And very, very tired. But then, from deep in the pit of
her gut there was something cheering. She pushed away her
mental to-do list and let herself savor the delicious sensation
of victory.

"Anna Simmons," she murmured through her smile. "Top
of the world."

Part of her wanted to dance around and cheer. She wanted
to kick off her heels and leap around on the dark leather fur-
niture. She had done it. She had pulled it together. Again.
Goddess Sportswear had just agreed to pay Arsenal Advertising a *fortune* for the fall campaign.

But she was exhausted. Dancing and cheering would have
to wait until she had had six straight hours of sleep. She did,
however, manage a little jump and a little wiggle on her way
over to her mahogany desk. Humming ABBA's "Dancing
Queen" under her breath she sat down at her desk. The chair
rolled around a little on the hardwood floor and she turned
it into a spin as she opened the bottom drawer and took out
the family size bag of Reese's Peanut Butter Cups she kept
stashed there for just these sorts of occasions.

She swivelled in her chair and faced her floor-to-ceiling
windows looking out over San Francisco Bay. She kicked off

her shoes and put her feet up on the printer table to survey her kingdom. Lights were beginning to illuminate the fading day. The houses on the hills of Sausalito were glowing with their pastel colors like Easter eggs and the Golden Gate Bridge was bloody red in the last bright rays of the sun.

A chuckle of contentment bubbled up from her chest.

Anna liked the birds the best. They looked like hundreds of bright white handkerchiefs blowing in the breeze. She watched them, ate her chocolate and knew that nothing could ruin her tremendous good mood.

There was a knock on her door and she turned toward it as Camilla Lockhart, her boss, mentor and friend, poked her head in.

"Camilla," Anna said expansively. "Come in." Thrilled that Camilla had stopped by to congratulate her, she held out her bag of chocolate. "Can I interest you in a peanut butter cup? In celebration?" The idea of drinks, those Cosmopolitans came back to her. "Wait!" She stood up. "Let's go get a drink. It's Wednesday but, Lord knows, we deserve it."

"You sure do," Camilla smiled broadly and walked farther into Anna's office. She put her briefcase down on the couch. "But I came in for a chat." Camilla sat down in one of the deep green wing chairs facing Anna's desk and crossed her long thin legs at the knee. Anna looked at her and marveled at how absolutely gorgeous Camilla was. She had long silver hair and eyes as sharp and blue as the sky outside the window. Camilla was in her sixties and she looked like a woman twenty years younger.

"All right." Anna sat back down and smoothed the wrinkled hem of her best black suit. Anna had spent the past five hours in the boardroom in heavy negotiations and she looked like she had crawled out of a trench. Camilla had been in and out of the room—coming in like some kind of fairy godmother when Anna had needed her most—and she looked as fresh and unscathed as she had first thing this morning. She was a marvel that woman.

Anna touched her black hair, relieved it was still pulled back in the bun she had fashioned twelve hours earlier. Of course, considering the serious engineering system of bobby pins and hair spray, having the bun actually fall out would take an act of God.

Anna's good mood was far too strong to be daunted by something like Camilla's unwrinkled suit. She dug back into her candy. "Let's chat about how unbelievably well today went."

Let's chat about how I kicked major ass! She thought but didn't say.

Camilla tilted her head, "I have to hand it to you, you were right about Goddess."

"Goddess just needed to be refocused," Anna said about the women's sportswear line. It had taken a few years to get Aurora Milan and her company to this place, but the effort was worth it. Goddess was about to explode all over the nation, Anna was sure of it. It wasn't the biggest deal in Arsenal history, but Anna was sure that it was the most important. "It's a great product with a great philosophy. It just needed some help getting out there."

"And that's where you come in." Camilla smiled.

Anna shook her head. "That's where Arsenal comes in."

"You did a great job," Camilla said, her eyes and smile warm. "I was very proud of you."

Anna nodded, uncomfortable, and tried not to show how outrageously pleased she was by Camilla's praise. There was this bubble in her chest, like a laugh trapped in her rib cage. "Well," she said, nodding, "I just did exactly what you taught me."

Camilla chuckled wryly, "Honey, in my best days I couldn't have pulled off that deal—"

"Not true," Anna interrupted, shaking her head. She

knew all of Camilla's victories. Sitting at the woman's right hand in that boardroom all these years had been the best education she could have wished for. "Norway Vodka," she said the name of one of their biggest clients who, long ago, had paid an unprecedented amount for Arsenal's advertising magic. Camilla had taken an almost unknown product and made it the most exclusive and high-end vodka in the world.

"Well." Camilla smiled and flicked imaginary lint off the hem of her red power suit. "That was a good one."

"See, Camilla—" Anna sat back and put her arms out expansively "—I just learned from the master. Of course, it doesn't hurt that Jennifer worked her tail off for the last week."

"Yes, she did." Camilla brushed back a lock of silver hair and took a breath. "But, Anna, no one else has spent the past two weeks sleeping on that couch." Camilla tilted her head toward the couch along the wall of Anna's office.

"Tell me about it," Anna said with a laugh. "It might be the most uncomfortable couch on the planet."

Camilla looked at Anna for a long second and Anna suddenly felt something else in the air. This was a time for laughs and pats on the back. Camilla didn't look much like laughing.

"What's wrong?" Anna put down the bag of candy and leaned on her desk.

"Well, Anna, I was going to wait and make an announcement in a few weeks, but I don't think things can wait that long." Camilla stood and walked over to the windows. She was a thin red line against the backdrop of the city. And Anna had the strange and terrible feeling that change was in the air. She wasn't a big fan of change.

"Oh, my God." Anna stood up. As a rule she jumped to the worst conclusions. It always seemed to get to the heart of the matter. There was very little beating around the bush in Anna's life. "You're sick."

"No," Camilla said quickly with a reassuring smile. "I am healthy, my family is healthy..."

"But?"

"I am retiring after the New Year."

Anna collapsed back hard into her chair. She had no idea what to say. Arsenal was Camilla's company, built out of a spare room in her house twenty-five years ago. Camilla had created, built and nurtured one of the biggest advertising agencies in the city. Even more, Anna felt like Camilla had created, built and nurtured her right along with the company. Anna had started working for Camilla ten years ago as a receptionist and now, she was sealing the deals that would ensure the future of the company. But Camilla was leaving. It was all just too much to take in.

"Anna," she said firmly and Anna's eyes darted back to her face. "It's not the end of the world."

"I know," she tried to relax. "It's just a surprise. But...why are you leaving? You're at the top of your game."

"No, sweetheart, *you* are at the top of your game. I'm just tired." Camilla chuckled but Anna couldn't find anything funny in this situation.

"What...?" Anna couldn't help feeling lost. She looked down at her fingernails and wanted nothing more than to bite them. "What about Arsenal?"

Camilla shrugged. She looked back out the window, her face in profile against the fading blue California sky, and tried to hide a smile. "I think you'll take good care of it."

"Me?" Anna asked, floored.

"You." Camilla turned to face her and Anna could feel the explosions going off in her head. Fireworks and cannons.

Holy shit! Anna Simmons, president of Arsenal Advertising. It was a dream come magically true.

Anna leaped up, grabbed Camilla around the waist and

squeezed, lifting her off the ground in her crazed enthusiasm. "This...oh, my God...I..." She was stuttering and laughing and at some point she felt herself crying. It was all just too much.

The day. Goddess. And now this, president of Arsenal. Camilla trusted her enough, believed in her enough to give this to her. Anna could hardly make sense of it all.

"Drinks, definitely drinks!" Anna said, laughing. "Cosmopolitans for everyone!"

"I'm glad you're so excited, but there's something we need to talk about first." Camilla put her cool hands on Anna's flushed face and made her look at her. Really look at her.

"Okay," Anna said carefully, the crazy joy subsiding in her chest. Something else was sneaking in, something that felt like dread. Camilla looked worried. Nervous and sad.

Uh-oh.

"Please sit down," Camilla said, gesturing with elegance and poise to the chair Anna had erupted from just minutes ago. Anna sat and, without thinking, grabbed the bag of chocolate while Camilla perched on the corner of the large mahogany desk.

"What's going on, Camilla?" Anna asked. "My heart can't take all this in one day."

"I am very excited about leaving you Arsenal. I believe in you and I trust you...."

The pause. The dreaded pause. Anna felt panic like a wave in her throat. *Why is she pausing there, she believes in me. Trusts me. No pauses!*

"But..."

"No, Camilla no buts..."

"But," Camilla talked over her. "I can't in good conscience allow you to take over the company the way you are right now."

Anna jerked, baffled. "What does that mean? The way I am right now?"

"It means you are killing yourself for this company and, at the rate you are going, if I give you Arsenal, you will be dead before you are forty."

"I have no idea what you are talking about," Anna said. The hard work, the weeks on the couch, the stress of the past five hours and now this... Anna felt a headache blooming behind her eyes. She pinched her nose.

"I know you don't." Camilla leaned forward. "For months I have been trying to get you to take a break. A vacation..."

"I will, I know," Anna sighed, relieved. This was just about a vacation. "Tomorrow. I promise. I'll book a cruise. I'll book two cruises. I just had to get this job..."

"Sweetheart, there is always a job. That's the nature of this business."

"Right, so...?"

"So, I've taken this upon myself."

"You've booked me on a cruise?" Anna asked, confused.

"No, but that's not a bad idea." Camilla seemed to consider it for a split second and then she pushed the silver hair off her face and took a bracing breath. "Until I retire in six months, you are, in essence, fired."

Anna blinked. Her mouth opened, words rushed through her brain but died in her throat. She shut her mouth. Opened it again. "Wh-what? What do you mean fired?"

"I mean you will not be working for six months. It's a forced, but paid, sabbatical."

The explosions from earlier came back. Canons in her head. And not the good kind. "Are you joking?" She started laughing incredulously. "Because I have to say, if you are, good one. Really. You had me going." She shook her finger at Camilla.

"I am not joking."

"Then I must have fallen asleep on the couch again, because there is no way—" disbelief had her on her feet "—*no way* the woman who just cemented the future of this company for you is getting fired!"

"Anna, sit down," Camilla urged calmly.

Anna sat. "Tell me this isn't real, Camilla. Please."

Camilla's unlined patrician face fell and she stood up. "It's very, very real and it's for your own good."

She was elegant and calm and as serene as she was in every situation. It was the end of Anna's world and Camilla might have been ordering lunch.

Anna's eye started to tick uncontrollably.

"Listen to me," Camilla said. "You have six months. A sabbatical."

"I don't want a sabbatical," Anna spat.

"Well, that's too bad, sweetheart, because you need one."

"I don't need one!"

Camilla's lips pursed for a second. "Anna," she said carefully. "Yesterday you threatened to shove chopsticks up Andrew's nose."

Well, Anna slouched a little bit in her chair. She had been working hard, she had been stressed out and Andrew, the little rat, had thrown out her leftovers. Perhaps holding the chopstick to his throat that way might have been a little much, but...

"Okay, that was too much," Anna admitted. "But that hardly translates into me needing six months off. Camilla, this is crazy."

"It's six months off. You come back and Arsenal is all yours. It's your company. President, just like we agreed."

"What if I say no?" Anna asked, her brows furrowed and the pain behind her eye nearly blinding. This was a nightmare. This day should have been a celebration and now it was hell.

"Then you're fired for real," Camilla told her in dead seriousness and Anna felt her heart stop for a moment. "You need these six months to get a life."

"I have a life!" Anna protested, hotly.

"Really?" Camilla asked and the pity in her eyes sent Anna to her feet. The chair spun out behind her and hit the glass of the window.

"Yes, *really*, this company is my life." Anna slammed the bag of candy on her desk. "I have devoted everything to Arsenal, every single thing...."

"That's the problem, sweetheart," Camilla said, standing to face Anna.

"How can that be a problem?" Anna was beginning to shout and she didn't care at all, which if she had been rational, would have alarmed her. "In this business, my kind of devotion is usually rewarded."

"Sit down, Anna," Camilla said in her persuasive tone usually reserved for tough clients.

"No!" Anna refused. "I won't sit down, Camilla. Not while you stab me in the back." Anna began to pace the small distance between the windows and Camilla. "Does this have anything to do with my job performance?"

"No," Camilla sighed and settled back down on Anna's desk. "You do an excellent job."

"Excellent, not just good. Not just fair, but an excellent job." Anna's finger jabbed the air right in front of Camilla's nose. It wasn't the job that drove Anna. Surely, Camilla could see that it was the excellence she was after. It was the details. It was perfection.

How does a perfectionist get fired?

"Yes."

"So excellent in fact..."

"Anna." Camilla crossed her arms over her chest, indicating her temper was wearing thin. "How many times have I come into the office in the morning and found out you spent the night on your office couch?"

"What does that have to do with anything?" Anna shrieked, unable to see the correlation.

"How many?" Camilla asked her voice cutting the air.

"A few," Anna answered throwing up her hands.

"Three hundred and sixty-two times."

"So?"

"What was the last play you saw? The last concert or movie?" Camilla continued.

"I just saw the new Brad Pitt movie!" Anna said, trying not to sound to triumphant.

"Brad Pitt hasn't been in a movie in two years," Camilla pointed out.

"Brad Pitt shouldn't have any kind of bearing on my job," Anna cried then shook her head. "Do you see how nuts all of this is? I must have fallen asleep at my desk, because this can not be real."

"How many dates have you been on in the last two years?" Camilla asked relentlessly.

"A few," Anna answered trying not to appear uncomfortable. That was a bit personal. And frankly, her love life was seriously...well, *non-existent* probably best covered it. But that hardly had anything to do with her job.

"Three. Three blind dates that I set you up on. Brent, Charles and Luke. Three nice, handsome and successful men that you completely rejected out of hand."

"Well, I didn't totally reject that Luke guy," Anna mumbled, feeling a blush creep up her throat.

"Anna, I am not talking about getting drunk and mauling some guy in the back of a cab."

"How'd you...?" she asked, feeling like a sixteen-year-old caught by her mother.

"Marie told me." Of course. Anna's sister who couldn't keep a secret to save her life.

"I took a date to Jeanie and John's wedding," Anna protested, talking about a coworker's wedding earlier in the year.

"You took your next-door neighbor who is gay!"

"I don't understand..."

"Besides Jim, have you ever had a man in your life for longer than one dinner?"

Anna's mouth fell open. Jim Bellows. Camilla was really reaching to be bringing up Jim. Anna had dated Jim when she first started working at Arsenal as a receptionist. They broke up when Anna started getting promoted. "Is this about a boyfriend? Because I think Jim proved that this job isn't all that conducive to relationships."

"The way you *do* the job isn't conducive to relationships." Anna opened her mouth to defend herself, but Camilla kept talking. "When was the last time you did something, anything that was fun?"

"I do fun things all the time," Anna answered, even as the words came out of her mouth she knew she was lying and that it would be only one more nail in the coffin Camilla was making for her. The coffin she was going to have to spend six months in.

"Anna." Camilla's tone softened and Anna's backbone stiffened in response.

"Fine, have it your way. I quit." She jabbed her finger at Camilla. "I don't want to have anything to do with an organization that treats its hardest workers like this."

Part of Anna had believed Camilla would quail under this threat. She had a half-baked notion of Camilla taking it all back and offering her the president position immediately.

But Camilla's eyebrow arched in the silence and Anna felt sanity slipping right out of the room.

"I could get a job anywhere," Anna shouted and Camilla's other eyebrow arched. "Don't play with me, Camilla."

"I know Mernick and Simon would kill to have you...."

"That's right, Mernick and Simon and a dozen other companies," Anna shot in.

"Is that what you want?" Camilla asked softly.

"It's the only choice you're giving me." Anna couldn't believe this conversation was continuing.

"Look, I'm giving you six months. If you want to go to another company, fine. You want to forget about all the work you put in here, go right ahead. Andrew will have every one of your accounts. You can say goodbye to Goddess Sportswear."

Ouch. Camilla really knew how to kick a girl when she was down, which used to be one of the things Anna kind of admired about her. It wasn't so pretty being on the receiving end of that honesty, however. Goddess Sportswear was Anna's baby, her very own. She had cultivated Aurora Milan, a ditzy woman with a good idea, had spun her designs into what was going to be the leading sportswear line for women in the country. In turn, Goddess would cement Arsenal's future.

Anna hung her head for a moment, overwhelmed by the sudden changes Camilla was making with her life.

"Or you can take six months off and come back and all of this will be yours." Camilla gestured at the view and the office and kingdom she had built and was ready to lay at Anna's feet. After six months. "I'm not playing with you." Camilla took a tentative step forward and Anna held her ground but she knew her expression must have been dark because Camilla stopped a safe distance away. "I'm trying to save you Anna. If you continue to work like this and take over Arsenal, you'll never have the opportunity to enjoy your life. You'll work yourself right into the grave with nothing to show for it but a bunch of advertising campaigns for sports bras and vodka." Camilla braved a step closer and Anna, feeling the walls close in on her, growled low in her throat. "Sweetheart, don't you want a family?"

Anna felt something sharp twist in her chest and she tried to ignore it. She had been ignoring that twist more and more over the past year and had, in fact, become a pro at pretending that there wasn't some internal clock ticking away inside her body. She had blocked off the part of her brain that had started counting the years that were flying by. If she noticed that all the women she knew her age were married, some with kids, she quickly rationalized it with her career. Some women chose family and some women chose career. Anna had made her choice and if sometimes that choice seemed a little lonely, then she only had to look at one of the million billboards or magazine ads for Goddess Sportswear to feel vindicated.

Besides, she was no good at family. She was good at Arsenal.

"You have to trust me," Camilla was saying. "This is for your own good."

Anna took a deep breath and turned to face her window and the view of the harbor and mountains behind it. The birds. She knew every single detail by heart. She had been looking at that view for fourteen hours or more a day for almost five years, ever since she'd moved into the office from her cubicle.

It had taken many long years to get from her spot behind the receptionist desk to this view.

Ten years of service to this woman and her company and this is where I end up. Anna shook her head.

Feeling empty and lost, she looked around her office, the familiar bland artwork and the pictures of her sister Marie, some of Camilla's kids and the one grandchild that she had gotten close to over the years. Those few pictures were really the only things that made her office different from any other office in any other building in any other city.

Looking at her desk, nothing surprised her, nothing was not just as she had left it. She knew what every file contained, what was in each stack of paper set at right angles. Her pens lined up across the top of her desk blotter. Her phone with the egg timer beside it that she used to keep herself on schedule. Because once you got off schedule, there was no going back.

This was her life. Her whole entire life.

"I think I hate you," Anna told her friend as she unwrapped another piece of chocolate and shoved it into her mouth. "Really, I think I hate you."

"I expected as much." Camilla pushed off the desk and reached into the briefcase she brought into Anna's office before dropping this bomb. She pulled out a stack of papers and looked through them idly.

"How can you so calmly ruin my life and still look like a woman in a makeup ad?" Anna asked, digging into her bag of candy again. "It's not right, Camilla. In fact, as I think about it, it's sick. How does this happen?"

"Anna, I am thirty years your senior and for a while I worked as hard as you do right now. But I always had a man standing right behind me, helping me out." She was, of course, referring to Michael, her husband and the father of their three children. "Being loved and helped and cared for when I needed it has made all the difference in my life."

So beyond caring, Anna put a finger down her throat and made a gagging sound, then bit into her chocolate.

"Then I got you," Camilla said and Anna looked up surprised. "I didn't have to work as hard because you were working hard enough for the both of us."

"Damn straight," Anna said with her mouth full.

"As a result, I feel a little responsible for the way your life is going."

"I like the way my life is going," Anna shouted and when chocolate flew out of her mouth she didn't even care.

This is how low a person can sink in the span of an hour, Anna thought wiping the chocolate off the highly polished surface of her desk.

"We'll see, Anna." Camilla looked at the thin watch on her wrist. "It's eight o'clock. You need to pack your things."

Anna heaved a big sigh. She put the candy back down, beginning to feel a little bit sick and pulled out her briefcase. When she started to put her files into her bag, Camilla stopped her.

"No work," she said.

"Who's going to take care of Goddess?"

"Andrew," Camilla said.

Anna saw red. "You're giving Goddess *to Andrew?*"

"I'll be advising, it's going to be fine."

"What about Bluetech and Norway Vodka and Frederick's?" Anna asked after her other major clients.

"Andrew and I can handle it," Camilla nodded her head once. "Keep packing."

Anna looked at Camilla for a moment in real disbelief and then didn't even try to hide it when she started muttering things about Camilla under her breath.

"My mother has nothing to do with this," Camilla said, but she was smiling. Anna collected her personal digital assistant, cell phone and pager to put in her bag, but again Camilla stopped her.

"You won't need those," she said.

"What am I allowed to take?" Anna asked, throwing her hands up again.

"Well, you can take those oranges you've got in your desk and that candy. It will probably be the only food you have in your house."

"Fine. Great. You know, as I think about this, this is a great idea. Six months away from your manipulations will serve me a world of good." Anna went to the small closet in her office. She opened the door and pulled out the suits hanging there. There were several, for those odd times that she slept on the couch.

"I'm sure it will." Camilla was still smiling and Anna snarled as she shoved her tailored suits, all black and expensive, into her very large briefcase. "But you'll be seeing me," Camilla said.

"Probably not," Anna answered over her shoulder as she went back to the closet for the toiletry bag she kept there. "I'll probably be too busy getting married and having children and learning how to knit to hang out with you," she growled. She grabbed the gym bag she used for her lunch-hour workouts, her blow-dryer, her contacts and spare glasses and the alarm clock.

"Well, actually." Camilla smiled and looked at the papers in her hand. "I realized that you wouldn't have the slightest idea how to actually get a life so I signed you up for some of the classes I take." Camilla flipped the papers. "And I made a list…"

"A list?" This was crazy. Camilla was accusing *her* of not having a life.

"A short one, just a few things I think you should do…."

"Maybe *you* need a sabbatical," Anna muttered.

"Starting," Camilla talked over Anna, "with the picnic we have on Monday for Memorial Day and Meg's birthday." Camilla referred to her oldest granddaughter; this was an event Anna usually missed for work.

Apparently not this year.

"You are worse than my mother," Anna said and didn't feel at all bad about what they both knew was a serious insult considering Anna's mother. But Camilla didn't even flinch. "At least she never kicked me out."

Anna shoved her extra blanket and the pillow into her gym bag and threw both bags over her shoulders. But they were so heavy that they fell a little bit and she ended up with them across her elbows, cutting off circulation to her hands. Her slippers fell out and she picked them up and carried them in her hand.

"This doesn't prove anything," she hissed when she saw Camilla laughing at all the stuff she kept at the office. But Camilla just smiled that enigmatic, could-be-a-model-for-Revlon smile. Anna grabbed the lists out of Camilla's hand and shoved them in the feet of her slippers.

"I'll be seeing you," Camilla called as Anna breezed out of the office.

Anna ignored her and held her head up high as she walked out of the place she had considered home for the past ten years of her life.

2

ANNA STABBED another piece of bread into one of the dips in front of her. She noticed, but certainly didn't care, that the roasted-red-pepper-whatever fell in huge globs onto the counter and onto her Donna Karan suit.

She shrugged and ate the bread in one bite. It was a few hours later and she still felt as though she was Chicken Little and the joke really was on her.

"Sis." Anna's sister Marie leaned against her oven and crossed her arms over her chest, ten bracelets arranged themselves on her wrists. "Take a breath. You're losing it. You didn't even taste those dips," Marie pointed out.

"Well, I'm too busy coming to grips with the total destruction of my life to notice hummus," Anna snapped. "I get to lose it. I am completely within my rights to lose it right now."

Marie blew out a breath and hung her head for a moment before crossing the kitchen to yank the piece of bread out of Anna's hand. "You have been here for an hour, you've eaten every carbohydrate I've got in my house. You've had half a bottle of wine and I still don't understand what's wrong."

Marie's long black curly hair fell over her shoulder, escaping from the scarf she was using to tie it back.

She looks like a gypsy, Anna thought a little glumly, her own self-esteem somewhere below sea level. *She looks like a gypsy and I look like...* Anna looked down at her probably ruined suit that was so terribly sensible and felt like her sister's shadow. Which, frankly, was nothing new. She yanked the piece of pita out of her sister's hand and ate it. Marie, who had spent most of the evening trying to be calm and sympathetic, finally cracked and laughed at Anna.

Get a grip, Anna told herself and mentally tried to rally.

"Okay, okay," Anna said. She swallowed and dusted off her hands. "I'm all right."

"There you go." Marie nodded her head and leaned against the other side of the counter where Anna was seated. They were in Marie's new apartment, her freshly painted orange kitchen. Not a color Anna would have picked, but somehow an orange kitchen totally suited Marie.

Marie picked up her glass of red wine and took a sip. "Now, let's talk about this rationally," Marie said. Anna chuckled, knowing those words had never come out of her sister's mouth. Rational and Marie were like oil and water.

"What have we got here, really?" Marie asked. She began cleaning up the mess of breadcrumbs and dip splatter that Anna had made in her whirlwind of stress eating.

"I've been fired for six months."

"Well, I imagine it's all in how you look at it. You think fired. I think...six months vacation." Marie shrugged. "Sounds like a dream to me."

"Imagine telling me to get a life and then handing me a list... I mean, what is she thinking?" Anna asked, not really listening to her sister. She was not dealing with this well, she knew that. She would feel calm for a second, then there would be an explosion in the back of her head and all she could think about was not going in to work tomorrow and how dumb it all was. How ridiculous. What was she supposed to do?

"Camilla is just looking after you like she always has." Marie walked back over to the sink and dumped the crumbs.

Anna laughed a dry little bark. "Couldn't she just slip me a twenty or...?"

"She's still doing that?" Marie asked, turning from the

sink surprised. "She never slips me twenties anymore."
When Anna had gotten a job at Arsenal at age eighteen, Marie had been sixteen. And when Camilla started taking Anna under her fine and gracious wing, Marie found a place there, too. Now both women looked at Camilla as someone much more than a boss or a friend. She was family of sorts, like a favorite aunt and it made the pain of this six-month betrayal even worse.

"No, no twenties, but anything would be better than this," Anna said glumly. She fiddled with the breadbasket and because it was empty, she used her finger to scoop up more of the hummous she wasn't actually tasting and put it in her mouth.

"You work too much," Marie said, snatching the basket and dips away from her. "And frankly, it's not like you are really fired. You are being slightly overdramatic here and, as a woman with a fine appreciation for dramatic, I can tell you there is no need."

"Yeah, but do you know what can happen in six months?" Anna asked her sister. "With Andrew in charge of Goddess, I may not have a company to run when this little vacation is over."

"Come on, Camilla is going to be there," Marie said skeptically.

"Sure, but she hasn't been a part of the day-to-day life of Arsenal in years."

"Anna," Marie interrupted sharply. "Do not sell that woman short."

Anna blew out a big breath and rolled her eyes. Camilla was hardly the one who needed to be defended here. Anna was the injured party, why couldn't her sister see that?

Marie poured more wine in her glass. "What's really got you so upset?" Marie asked quietly.

"You mean it's not enough that life as I know it is over?" Anna asked and took a sip of her wine. Marie hummed and leaned on the counter. "It's not enough that the fall line for my pet project is going to be run by a spineless imbecile?" Anna was working herself up; she could feel her heart rate doubling. "How about I really have no idea what she wants me to do? What am I supposed to do for six months?"

"How about sleep?" Marie suggested.

"I sleep," Anna protested, but Marie obviously didn't believe her. "Okay, so I sleep for a week, then what. *Get a life?* I don't have any idea what she means."

"That—" Marie lifted her glass and looked over the edge at Anna "—is the saddest thing I have ever heard." Marie drank and the buzzer on the stove went off. She turned around to deal with what had become a very elaborate midnight snack.

Anna sat in her barstool and felt lost. She felt as though she was eighteen years old and her mother was leaving all over again. What was with the older women in her life abandoning her like this? Just when she felt like she was accomplishing things, someone she loved and trusted ripped the world out from under her feet. Get a life? It made no sense.

"So," Marie was saying as she pulled a casserole dish out of the oven. The air filled with the smells of oregano, basil and buttery pastry crust. Despite having eaten everything within arm's reach, Anna was starving. "You do what she needs you to do. You read some books, take naps, help your sister renovate." Marie looked merrily out of the corner of her eye at Anna.

"You can't take my lemons for your lemonade," Anna laughed ruefully, but the gorgeous tart Marie was putting on the counter to cool distracted her. "What is that?"

"Tomato and basil tart," Marie said and pulled out some dishes. "I am thinking of adding it to the menu at Marie's."

Tired and sad and lost and hungry, Anna looked at her sister buzzing around her kitchen and felt a sudden deep appreciation for her. Marie had finally moved back to San Fransico a few months ago and, after working in others' kitchens for most of the past eight years, she had figured out, as Anna knew she always would, that she was not a good employee. She put down her savings on a little restaurant in a funky new area of town and was planning on taking the San Francisco dining world by storm. And she would, Anna was sure of it. Marie took everything by storm.

Not like Anna, she thought bitterly. *Anna gets fired.*

With a groan she put her head on the counter. She had not set out in this world to be an advertising executive. But she was one. A damn good one. And the only place in the world that she wanted to be was Arsenal.

Her childhood had been filled with a hundred moves. A thousand little changes over that span of years that made Anna feel as though her whole life was built on quicksand. The only concrete thing, the only real thing besides her sister was Arsenal. Ten years of work and steadfast devotion to the woman who gave her a chance to build her life and the odd twenty dollar bill when things got tight.

She had just gotten to a place with Goddess that would ensure Arsenal would always be in her life. It was all she wanted, something real to keep her going.

"Oh, come on," Marie laughed. "You know, I still remember the day when you told Mom you weren't going to move away with her again." Marie was leaning against the counter again. Anna sighed heavily hoping to push away the pain that always accompanied that particular memory.

"She had that crappy car, that..." Marie paused, trying to remember.

"Hatchback," Anna supplied, her voice muffled as her head was still on the counter.

"She had gotten fired again, remember? And we were going to go south...some relative that we hadn't already hit up...."

"Her aunt in Arizona," Anna said.

The memory was there, no point in trying to push it away. Anna, Marie and their mother, Belinda had lived in a tiny one-bedroom apartment off Haight-Ashbury—an apartment that smelled constantly of fried chicken and wet dogs. But they had stayed in that place for a year. Anna finished her whole senior year there. She made friends. Sort of. She fell in love with California. With staying put. When Belinda had come home and said they were moving again, Anna felt sick. And she felt very mad. Her mother was so lazy, she would rather leave than do what it took to keep a job and stay. There was always a free lunch someplace else.

"It's the last time," Belinda had told them and Anna knew her mother believed it. Belinda if nothing else had faith and that faith had kept them going for years. Through small towns and big cities, East Coast and West Coast. Endless "uncles" and "friends." Endless crappy one-bedroom apartments.

Belinda fed them faith and, hungry for anything, Marie and Anna ate it.

But that day when Anna and Marie walked out of the dumpy apartment into the cool and sweet-smelling California air, Anna took one look at her mother who was so willing to destroy the fragile roots she had put down, and Anna set down her bag.

She had no more room in her stomach for faith.

"I'm eighteen and I'm staying," she had said.

Anna lifted her head from Marie's counter and found her sister smiling at her. "I thought you were nuts then," Marie told her quietly.

"Well, you got in the car with her," Anna laughed, though the memory felt like rocks in her stomach.

"But I came back a month later," Marie whispered.

Anna's smile was wide and real and she reached out to pat Marie's head. "The best day ever was when I opened my door and there you were sitting on your old suitcase."

"What did I say?" Marie asked, because this was an old game for them. As two women against the world, they traced their connections.

"Arizona is hot," Anna repeated. They both smiled.

"You are the woman who found us places to live when we had no money." Marie reached out and twined her fingers with Anna's. "You got me through high school and yourself through college. You kept us in oranges and peanut butter cups. There's nothing more you have to prove, Anna. Take a break. So, you take some yoga classes, you meet Camilla for tea. Big deal. This has nothing to do with your worth as a person. This is about you relaxing. You can do anything you set your mind to. This is a cakewalk to someone like you."

Set your mind to it.

She sighed heavily as she understood Marie was right. She had certainly survived worse things than getting a life. She would just have to put her mind to it. The heart was a messy organ, tears and hummous everywhere. Anna's brain, however, was well used to cleaning up the mess.

Put your mind to it. Exactly.

"What I need," Anna said, slowly realizing that this wasn't a complete disaster. It certainly wasn't going to be as hard as creating Goddess Sportswear out of a crazy woman's daydreams. It wasn't going to be as hard as paying her sister's way through culinary school. It wasn't going to be as hard as watching her mother drive away for the last time. "Is a plan," she said, dusting crumbs off her hands.

She thought hard for a few moments trying to create a to-do list. She tried to give herself a clear objective. A task. But there was nothing there. Just day after day of tea and yoga.

"It's going to be okay, Anna, you'll see." Marie slid a plate filled with tart and salad in front of her.

Anna shrugged and dug in. She felt better. Not great, but better. Part of her still believed she was very small in this world and the sky was, in fact, falling.

ON THE FIRST DAY of unemployment Anna was staring up at the ceiling over her bed at 5:30 a.m. There were thirty-two cracks in her ceiling that she had never noticed before and if she stared at them long enough—which she had been doing since five o'clock—the cracks started moving, making shapes, spelling words.

Right now the cracks were spelling "get a life." It was better than the "loser" she'd read there at 3:00 a.m.

She flopped over onto her stomach and closed her eyes trying hard to fall back to sleep.

You're unemployed, she thought. *You can sleep all day.*

After a few moments of trying to call up sheep to count, Anna gave up and flopped back over on her back, considering as she had been since yesterday evening, what exactly "getting a life" entailed.

She still lived in the first apartment she'd moved into after she could afford to get her and Marie out of that smelly one-bedroom up on Haight. Marie had just graduated and Anna had gotten a promotion from receptionist to Camilla's assistant. Marie, instead of sticking around, had decided to go to Texas. *Or was it Minnesota?* Anna wondered.

Well, whichever it was, Anna was still rattling around in an ancient, one-story, two-bedroom condo close to University of California at Berkley because she'd had no time to even look for a new place. But the apartment suited her. She was very rarely here anyway.

Maybe it's time to move on, Anna thought. *Maybe I should buy a house.* The soft pastel houses of Sausalito lit up her brain for a moment, but Anna quickly got rid of that idea. A house meant commitment and upkeep and responsibility. Maybe she'd think about it when this sabbatical was over, but right now she simply wasn't ready to make those kind of long-term changes.

No matter what Camilla wanted.

Cosmetic changes, that's what she was looking for. She

liked her life as it was and she would jump through Camilla's hoops long enough to get back to that life, while giving the *appearance* of change without really changing. Smoke and mirrors. Anna smiled just thinking about it.

Looking around, she realized she didn't have one single thing on the wall. Not a poster or a picture, not even a bulletin board. Nothing. She should get some home decor. Camilla had a modern art collection with some kind of weird chrome sculpture in her living room. Camilla had, at one time, tried to get Anna to care about the crap she had up on her walls but Anna had been occupied with Goddess Sportswear's quarterly numbers and, if she remembered correctly, she couldn't be bothered.

Anna grinned and decided she would take some time, which she had plenty of, and buy some crap that Camilla might like and put it on her walls.

"Step one," she told her ceiling. "Get crap."

See how easy this was going to be?

Camilla had long been telling Anna about the inherent relaxing and mind-expanding properties of "having a hobby." For Camilla a hobby was something entirely creepy, like pottery and Tai Chi. Those were two of the things on Camilla's list.

Anna grimaced at the idea of all those weirdos in the park swaying in the breeze. And pottery? Who was Camilla kidding? A bunch of middle-aged women sitting around playing with mud. Anna would rather take up dentistry. She looked up at the ceiling. The hobby question would require more thought.

Anna let out a big sigh and reluctantly turned her mind to what she was sure was Camilla's big hang-up.

Don't you want a family?

A boyfriend. In Camilla's eyes Anna needed nothing more than a boyfriend to marry her and give her babies. Camilla had said so only about four million times in the years Anna had been at Arsenal.

"If I get a boyfriend—" Anna jabbed her finger at the cracks in the ceiling "—it's game over. I win."

A boyfriend. Anna didn't particularly want one. She certainly wouldn't mind some of the naked benefits that came with having a boyfriend. She wouldn't really even mind having someone to drink Sunday morning coffee with. In bed. And then some being naked.

That would all be fine. It was the other stuff Anna didn't want. She and Jim had had a fun and happy relationship for about a year. A year that she had thought was pretty normal. They went to movies, out to dinner. They laid on a blanket in the park on Sundays. She had *felt* normal, and while not exactly in love, she did like Jim. But as she got promoted at work, her job demanded more time and things between them fell apart and everything about Jim began to bother her.

He used to clean his ears and then put the Q-Tips in the toilet, but he wouldn't flush the toilet. It made Anna crazy. The sharing of space. The family obligations. The arguing over the amount of work Anna did. That was the stuff she could do without. That was the stuff she didn't have time for.

Poor Jim just didn't understand what Arsenal meant to her. And so Poor Jim had left. And that had been mostly okay with Anna.

Anna looked up at the cracked ceiling and frowned. Poor Jim had been *really* good with the naked stuff.

But Anna was looking for smoke and mirrors, not a relationship.

"Nope," she told the cracks in the ceiling. "A boyfriend at this point just isn't in the cards."

3

AT 6:30 A.M. ON THE FIRST DAY of her unemployment, Anna was eating one of the oranges from her office while she stood in front of her shut closet door, contemplating what was going to be behind that door. Two months ago her washing machine had broken down and she had stopped doing laundry except for the things that could be dropped off at the dry cleaners. Which was why she was now wearing a dark blue silk suit.

When the machine broke, she had called for someone to repair it, but that required her being home to let the guy in. Which, of course, had been impossible in the middle of the week. And considering her sometimes twenty-hour days, she could forget about hauling herself to the laundry room. So, for two months, instead of washing her underwear, she'd bought more on the internet.

Behind that closet door Anna guessed there might be close to a hundred pairs of dirty underwear. *And blue jeans*, Anna thought suddenly remembering that she actually owned some of those.

Anna popped another segment of orange in her mouth and considered getting a cleaning woman. After all, Camilla had one. And, Anna realized this morning as she looked around her place for the first time in what was probably months, there were things in her apartment covered in a thick fur of something that might be dust. She remembered that she had contemplated a cleaning woman a few months ago, but she just never had the time to straighten up before someone could come over to clean. Besides, Anna was not a big fan of a stranger being in her house, touching her things. So she had put it off and put it off, until like most things in her private life, she had forgotten all about it.

Perhaps she should invite Camilla over to watch her sweep the dust out from under her bed. Surely, that was life-getting at its best.

Putting the last segment of orange in her mouth she threw open the closet door and stood still in the small avalanche of dirty clothes that rolled out onto her feet.

"I wondered where those went," Anna said, looking down at a pair of khaki pants that she hadn't seen in months. "I thought I threw that out." She picked up an old U.S.C. sweatshirt that was stiff with whatever was growing on it. "Gross," she muttered and quickly dropped it.

Standing ankle-deep in clothes that had been stagnating in her closet Anna guessed that her first real effort in getting a life would be laundry.

She had a small plastic hamper, which was ridiculous in the face of all of her dirty clothes. Even her gym bag was too small. With a resigned sigh, she pulled her giant roller suit-case off the top shelf, put it on the floor and began shoving clothes into it. Halfway through, Anna started breathing through her mouth.

When all of her clothes were in the suitcase, she felt pretty good and decided there was nothing wrong with a Reese's Peanut Butter Cup for breakfast. After all she was unemployed. She didn't need to worry about getting a healthy breakfast.

After laundry, she would have to tackle the grocery store.

In the back of the closet, Anna found some laundry detergent. So, with her suitcase, a mouthful of chocolate and laundry soap that hadn't seen daylight in two months, Anna set out to find the building's communal laundry facility. She had been given a tour when she moved in. That was the last time she had seen it.

Before walking out the door she remembered quarters and grabbed the jar she kept on her dresser that was filled to overflowing with change.

Anna's apartment complex was huge, much bigger than she'd ever realized. There were pathways that seemed to go on for miles. Buildings she never knew existed were nestled in small hills and valleys that were actually quite pleasant, or would be if Anna wasn't wandering around in high heels dragging a heavy suitcase filled with dirty laundry. Her hand was beginning to cramp around the change jar, so she switched hands with the laundry soap and tried to drag the suitcase in her soap hand. For a few minutes it was okay, then that hand started to cramp. So she rearranged everything again.

Anna walked around lost for fifteen minutes, but finally she found the laundry room. After the bright sunlight, stepping down the small cement steps into the basement facilities was like stepping into a cave. It was cool and smelled like every laundromat she had been in with her mother and Marie over the years. That strange combination of detergent, fabric softener and cigarettes.

Anna looked around and noticed that all of the washing machines were open.

"Excellent," she mumbled. She unzipped her suitcase and began filling the washing machines with armloads of laundry.

Whoever lived in the apartment directly above or perhaps to the right of the laundry room apparently loved Celine Dion and seemed to have a hearing problem. Anna could hear the singer clearly through the wall and as she dumped soap and clothes into every washing machine she started bobbing her head in time. She wasn't a huge fan of the woman, but she played on the radio every ten seconds.

And she recognized the song currently playing and sang along—Celine Dion style, adding some chest pounds for the hell of it. And for the moment, Anna didn't mind at all being unemployed. She was busy, she had some tasks, there was an agenda and it was early. After the day she had had yesterday she would take what she could get.

Walking back to her suitcase and the jar of coins, she saw a sock she had dropped on the floor and she bent to pick it up. She twirled with a little flourish in time with the music and pitched the sock toward the last open washing machine. It went in and because she was in a good mood and the air smelled clean and no one was in the room, she lifted her arms turning her silly dance into a victory dance.

"Excuse me?"

Anna screamed, startled and whirled toward the deep voice behind her. "Holy…" she breathed, her hand at her chest. "You scared me."

A man was standing on the step leading into the small laundry room. He was backlit by the bright sunshine and in the relative darkness of the room she couldn't see him clearly. But she saw he was big. Tall and wide. Not fat.

"Sorry," the man said and though Anna couldn't see his face, she guessed he was smiling. He sounded like he was smiling. He was a big, wide, smiling man. Anna felt her day improve a little more.

"No problem," she said as her heart rate went back to normal. "I…well, I thought I was alone."

"Obviously," the guy said.

Obviously? Anna thought, her brows snapping together before she reminded herself that he could see her. *What the hell does that mean?*

"The dancing gave it away," he said and Anna ridiculously felt herself blush. He should have ignored that. Pretended he didn't see her dancing around to some teenager's music. Polite people pretended they didn't see people do embarrassing things. "The singing, too," he added with a chuckle.

Wow. He's laughing at me. A few choice words about spying and the difference between polite and rude rose to her tongue. Then, tall wide man stepped out of the doorway into the laundry room and Anna's brain shut down.

Oh. My. God. Anna thought. He was easily the most handsome man Anna had ever seen in real life—short blond hair, green eyes that even in the darkness of the laundry room seemed to glow. He looked down at his laundry then up at her and his eyes seemed to touch her and she felt the strange chill of awareness creep up her back and across her chest. He was still smiling and she could see it all there in his green, green eyes.

Her heart, usually so strong and steady, went *ka-thunk*.

All the rest of him—the bones, the skin, the stubble across his chin and cheeks, even the veins on his arms that every woman on the planet absolutely adored—combined to create some kind of Prince Charming. This man was what her mind would conjure up when she was a little girl and her mother read fairy tales to her and her sister. When the hero came cruising up on a white horse he looked like this guy.

She had forgotten all about that, but as she looked at him it all came back to her and she smiled.

His eyebrows lifted and the look in his eyes changed from merry to uncomfortable. "Hi."

Oh, God, stop staring, Anna told herself. "Hi." She smiled stiffly and turned away, feeling dumb.

Great, she thought as she grabbed her jar of change. *Prince Charming. Wonderful. Fairy tales, what is wrong with me? The man laughed at me.*

"Are you using all of the machines?" he asked as Anna shoved quarters in the washers. Anna shut the lid on the last one, put in a small fortune in coins and glanced around the room at all the washing machines quietly chugging away.

"Looks like it." She walked over to her suitcase and threw the detergent and the jar of coins into it.

"You didn't leave one open?" he asked and Anna looked up sharply at his tone. That tone was not a Prince Charming kind of tone and the look in his eyes was not nearly as merry as it had been a moment ago.

"I've already started all of them," she told him. "You could come back in—" she looked at the digital read out on the first machine she had started "—fifteen minutes."

"Since I've never seen you here before I am going to guess that you didn't see the sign."

He gestured with his thumb to a sign on the wall that she hadn't seen.

"Of course I've seen the sign," she huffed.

"Well, then you know." He obviously didn't believe her. *Smart-ass*, Anna thought. "You should leave one machine open."

"Who the hell are you?" Anna asked. "The laundry room police?"

"No, I'm a guy with no clean clothes," he snapped back.

"Look, I didn't think anybody else would be doing their laundry at—" she looked at the clock which was right by the sign she hadn't read "—8:00 a.m."

"Oh, I didn't realize I needed to run my laundry schedule past you."

Anna and Prince Charming had a little silent showdown. She guessed he expected her to apologize and haul a bunch of wet clothes out of a machine so he could wash some of his big, tall clothes. And perhaps she might have done that, if the man—a complete stranger—hadn't laughed at her. *Really, you don't laugh at strangers. It doesn't make you any friends.*

His eyes were boring into hers and, tired of him, she raised her eyebrows, well aware that there were few better stand-off enders than a properly raised eyebrow.

"Fine," he said, moving to the door. "But you could be a little more considerate."

"Jerk," she muttered under her breath.

"Bitch," he muttered back and she had heard it enough times that it barely even hurt.

IT TOOK ANNA four hours to do all of her laundry. Well, an hour of laundry and then three hours of folding and trying to figure out where to put all her clothes. She was able to avoid seeing Prince Charming again, which she was pretty happy about. Having cooled down, she realized she had acted childishly and didn't look forward to having to see him.

Anna was comfortably wearing clean underwear, freshly laundered jeans and a U.S.C. sweatshirt she thought she had thrown out. At the grocery store—the second item on her agenda today—she toyed with the idea of actually buying food to cook. Then she remembered who she was and bought some staples and a lot of microwave dinners.

She was unloading groceries back at her place when the phone rang.

She cradled the phone between her shoulder and ear while she opened the refrigerator door.

"Hello," she said, picking up the three bags of oranges she bought and dumping them onto one of the shelves.

"Anna?"

Anna stilled, the hair on the back of her neck pricked. She shut the refrigerator door and leaned against it.

"Hello, Camilla," she said smoothly.

"How is your first day of unemployment?" her boss asked brightly.

"Fabulous," Anna answered snidely. "I should have quit years ago."

Camilla only laughed at Anna's little dig.

"What do you want, Camilla?" Anna grabbed up the bags

of Reese's Peanut Butter Cups she had bought and fired them into a cupboard.

"I'm just making sure that you are going to be at the barbecue on Monday."

"I can't," Anna said quickly. "I'm busy."

"No, you're not."

"You don't know that," Anna snapped.

"Of course I do. Your sabbatical just started yesterday."

Anna put a jar of peanut butter and a loaf of bread in the fridge.

"I already told Meg you were going to be there. Marie will be there."

"That's a seriously low blow, Camilla." Anna blindly shoved a quart of milk into the cupboard.

"Well, sometimes low blows are the only ones that get things done," Camilla chuckled. "It's a barbecue with people who love you. It's not the Spanish Inquisition."

"Fine," Anna breathed. "I'll be there."

"Oh, Anna, I am giving you fair warning so that you don't freak out at the picnic..."

Just those words sent a chill to Anna's heart, those were words with trouble all over them.

"I've invited someone I would like you—"

"No, you didn't," Anna interrupted, knowing that this someone was a single man who Camilla was dying to fix her up with. "You did not do that, Camilla."

"Well, yes, I did. He's very nice. A doctor."

"I don't care. I don't care who he is. You have meddled enough with my life."

"It's not like I've set you up on a blind date. I just invited a nice single doctor—" Camilla put a little emphasis on the doctor part "—to my granddaughter's birthday party. There is nothing more to it than that."

But Anna knew better. With Camilla there was always something more. She was a Pandora's Box of more.

AFTER PUTTING all her food back in the right spots Anna was at a loss. What did unemployed people do all day? She collapsed onto her couch. She was wide-awake so taking a nap would be fruitless. She checked her watch and thought longingly of the meeting she would be attending if she were at Arsenal.

But she wasn't at Arsenal and thinking about it would just depress her. She dug the remote control out from under her butt and decided she would discover the joys of daytime television.

A half hour later she threw the remote back on the couch and decided there was no joy to daytime television.

People, she thought, *shouldn't sleep with amnesia victims who might be relatives. It's gross.*

Anna stood up and decided to clean her apartment. She had cleaned plenty of apartments. She had picked up after her messy sister and mother, so she was no stranger to the mop and broom.

But this. This was very much beyond her. She quickly realized that what had become of her home was something best left to a professional. The basics, sweeping and mopping she could handle. It was the advanced cleaning, the things involving mildew and harsh chemicals, that were destroying her apartment. She'd already accidentally bleached part of her carpet and the paint was bubbling up from the wall in her kitchen where she had sprayed the wrong kind of cleaner.

She quickly called a cleaning service and scheduled someone to come deal with the disaster. But in the mean time, the bathroom with its sturdy tile proved to be less destructible so she tried to tidy that up.

She was on her hands and knees in the tub working at the brown stuff around the drain when the solution to her problem—no, not the brown stuff problem. The other, bigger problem. The getting a life problem—hit her. Like a lightning bolt.

What better way to thwart Camilla and this doctor than to show up with a date of her own?

She sat straight up, the toothbrush in her hand dripped onto her jeans.

She needed a date, but not just any date. She needed a man who would expect no romantic entanglements. A man she wouldn't have to exchange small talk with or any other uncomfortable platitudes.

"Gary," she said with a smile.

She climbed out of the tub, threw the gloves and the toothbrush in the sink and headed out the door for Gary's apartment.

Gary was perfect as a date-on-call for several reasons.

1. He lived just around the corner in her condo complex.

2. He was a mostly out of work actor and he had viewed the wedding she took him to as a chance to be on stage, which was why halfway through the night people were expressing their condolences for the brain tumor Gary was telling people he had.

3. He was gay. There were absolutely no uncomfortable entanglements.

In a word: perfect.

Anna crossed the small stretch of grass between her unit and his with a glad heart. She was going to beat Camilla at her own game. Anna laughed a little bit thinking about how perfect this was. How truly satisfying it would be to get back at Camilla in just this exact way.

Gary had been leaving messages on her machine for the past two weeks that she had not had the time to return and she felt a little bad. But he would understand. Gary was good like that.

The light was on behind his blinds, which Anna took as an omen that her plan was going to work out okay. She stepped up on his small cement landing and knocked. She felt bad that she hadn't seen him in so long, a few weeks anyway. He had gotten some part in a play and she, of course, was always busy, so time flew by. She smiled and knocked again, happy that she had more time to spend with Gary who was always fun.

She heard footsteps and for the first time in a while, felt a smile that wasn't forced spread across her face. She pushed back a lock of hair just as the door opened and she felt all the blood drain from her face.

"Well, well." Prince Charming leaned against the door frame and crossed his arms over his bare chest.

4

"YOU?" ANNA WAS far more than surprised. She felt oddly as though the bottom of her stomach was missing. The man who had been so handsome fully clothed was now shirtless...

"In the flesh."

"What are you doing here?" Anna asked. *Where is Gary? Is this guy a friend of Gary's? A...lover?*

"I live here."

Anna ignored his sarcasm. "Where's Gary?"

"Well, if you're talking about the guy who lived here before me, he moved out two *weeks* ago." Prince Charming idly scratched his chest, which of course, was hairless and perfect and distracting to Anna in a dozen different ways.

"Two weeks?" she repeated partly because she didn't believe it and partly because his abdomen had that six-pack effect that made women want to lick men's stomachs.

"Yeah, he got some part in a soap opera or a play or something. Listen, not that this isn't real fun standing here watching you watch me, talking about a guy you apparently didn't know very well, but I've got paint I'd like to watch dry."

"Wait a second, Gary moved?" The message on her machine. Of course, he was calling to tell her that he got the part and was moving. Anna, as per usual, was an awful friend. Anna's ruined dreams of petty revenge were not nearly as disappointing as the fact that she had missed saying goodbye to Gary. She ducked her head for a second feeling truly awful.

"Do you have his address or number?" she asked.

He looked at her carefully for a second, then nodded. "Just a second," he said. He pushed away from the doorframe and turned around. As the door shut behind him, she saw a long puckered scar that ran up the center of his back toward his hairline.

The scar was shocking. Brutal and ugly against the smooth, tan skin of his back.

"Oh, no..." she breathed as he walked away. She blinked and swallowed, not sure of what she had seen. Could this be any worse?

Nice one, Anna. Why don't you go door to door offending and alienating people? You're off to a great start. She felt horrible. Maybe she had spent too much time away from regular people. Dealing with the sharks in the advertising world had made her intolerant. Maybe, just maybe, she was a bitch. She'd threatened to kill Andrew with chopsticks. She'd lost touch with Gary and she was rude ' ɔ a complete stranger just because he caught her making a fool of herself.

She felt like she was ten years old again sitting on a playground at a new school all by herself. She remembered all the quiet, kind kids who had tried to reach out to the new girl and she had bitten off their hands because she didn't know what to do.

He came back within moments carrying a slip of paper. Anna took it and smiled up at him ruefully. "I was really rude to you. I am sorry." He remained silent and Anna tried again. "You caught me making an ass out of myself and it embarrassed me. I really am sorry."

There was a tense moment between them and it seemed like his very green eyes were looking right through her. She let him do it and, when he finally smiled at her, she felt like a weight had been lifted off her chest.

"Don't worry about it," he said and from the tone in his voice, Anna guessed that he had forgiven her for most of her stupid behavior. "I was pretty awful myself. We can call it even. I'm Sam. Sam Drynan."

"Hi, Sam, I'm Anna." She held out her hand and he shook it and, though she really couldn't believe it, certainly never heard of it occurring in real life, electricity zipped across her fingertips and up her arm from the contact.

What the…? She looked down at her hand nearly lost in the giant paw of his hand and wondered if maybe she had stepped into some sort of Meg Ryan movie. Electric touches did not happen in Anna's life.

"Is there anything else I can do for you?" He grinned. His thumb lightly stroked the flesh of her hand and Anna's stomach did a pleasant little shimmy.

Oh…what? That? Is he? Flirting! Anna pulled her hand out of his and he smiled warmly at her. He is! *He is flirting with me!*

Anna giggled and then quickly wanted to kill herself.

"No, that will be all." She cringed. "I mean that's all I need. Thanks."

"Are you a professional Celine Dion impersonator?" he asked.

"No, strictly amateur."

"Well, you've certainly got her moves down." She looked at him blankly before he lightly beat his chest with his fist.

"Right." She clapped her hands together in front of her so they wouldn't do anything stupid like try to touch him. "Well, you should see my Michael Jackson."

He laughed and she appreciated his sense of humor. *A funny guy*, she thought. *I like that in a total hunk.*

She stood there smiling at him, her body doing ridiculous things in reaction to just him being there. Shirtless and very handsome. Her thoughts about getting naked from the morning came back. Sam Drynan was definitely the kind of man she could get completely naked with.

"Well, um…" Anna realized she had been standing there,

staring silently for several seconds. "Yes, thanks for the number and um, again sorry about earlier and..." She nodded her head and started backing off the porch. "Yeah, that's it."

"Okay, you don't need anything else?" he asked, crossing his arms over that nice chest and leaning against the door frame. Anna shook her head, the power of speech suddenly abandoning her.

He lifted his hand in goodbye and shut his door. Anna started to walk back to her apartment. She stopped.

Camilla. The doctor. She sucked air in through her teeth and weighed the satisfaction of thwarting Camilla against the embarrassment of asking Sam out on a date. He was infinitely more effective than Gary. He was gorgeous and straight. More than that, he had flirted. She might be out of practice, but she wasn't a complete lost cause.

The fact was she had nothing to lose and just imagining the look on Camilla's face was enough to make her head back to Sam's door and knock.

"You need to borrow some quarters?" he asked, laughing as he opened the door.

"I need a date," she blurted. His mouth fell open and Anna wished that the ground would open right up and swallow her. "I mean, not a real date. A fake date." His eyebrows snapped together and Anna, in a panic of regret and embarrassment, just kept digging the hole. She was the kind of person who, once she made a mistake, could seem only to make it worse. It was why she tried to never make mistakes in the first place. But here she was trying to jam both feet in her mouth. "There's a doctor and Camilla and a picnic, well, a picnic and a birthday party..."

"You need two dates?" he asked.

"No!" she said. "Just one. It's a picnic and birthday party combined."

"For a doctor?"

"No, I'm trying to stay away from the doctor."

"Oh!" Understanding dawned on his face. "You need a decoy date."

That sounded a bit cold, but when a spade was a spade... "Yes, I need a decoy. I came by here to get Gary to go with me but..."

"He's moved." He nodded his head and Anna reminded herself that he had been flirting with her. She wasn't that out of practice. She wasn't that blind. Sam had shown definite interest and she was just doing what hundreds of women did everyday. She was asking a handsome man on a date. Well, a decoy date, but he seemed to understand.

"It's on Monday. Noon," she said into the very uncomfortable silence. "Memorial Day."

"Good day for a picnic." He was nodding again and the suspense was becoming almost too much. She was about to tell him to stick his six-pack and his lovely hairless chest right up his...

"I'll think about it, Anna," he said with a smile.

I'll think about it? He might as well say I'd rather date Don Rickles.

"Okay," she answered, feeling like an idiot.

She turned.

"Maybe you should leave me your number?" he said.

Right. Number. Duh. She turned around and told him her number before he could go back in and get a piece of paper or a pencil. Then she leaped down from the landing and walked across the grass, feeling the whole time the weight of his eyes on her back. *What the hell was that?* she wondered. *I'll think about it?* The man had stroked her hand with his thumb. *Men don't just do that, do they? Maybe they do. Maybe I am a complete loser.*

She almost went back and told him not to do her any favors, but in the end decided that there really was only so much embarrassment a girl could take in one day and she had hit her limit.

The last part of the day stretched ahead of her in one long yawn. A whole lot of absolutely nothing. How was she ever going to survive this sabbatical? Perhaps if she made an effort to make an ass of herself in front of a handsome guy every day, the time would just fly by.

Anna shook her head and shoved open the door to her apartment.

Maybe daytime TV improved the later it got in the day. She shrugged. It's not like she had anything better to do.

SAM DRYNAN watched Anna leave and couldn't quite decide what to do. He couldn't actually figure out who she was and why he even wanted to watch her walk across the manicured lawn that separated her unit from his.

She was partly a nightmare, that was certain. A bossy nightmare. But at the same time there had been a few seconds while watching her dance around the laundry room that he had been charmed. And then she had looked at him with those impossible blue eyes and wide genuine smile and he had thought, *Am I really this lucky? Do I get to walk into a laundry room and meet this girl?*

Then, of course, she'd opened her mouth and ruined the image.

She was gorgeous. Tall and thin with black hair that had been tied back in a sort of serious-looking bun. Mostly it was her eyes, so big and so blue, blinking up at him that had him wondering what he was doing. A woman with eyes that big and that blue could only be trouble.

He had had the same kick-in-the-gut feeling tonight when he opened the door and saw her there with the same smile. Of course, immediately after she asked him out as a decoy. Did she think he was nuts? Well, he was a little, clearly, because he was thinking about going with her.

Sam laughed and shook his head. He closed his front door and went back into his apartment. He walked to his kitchen and grabbed a bottle of water and leaned against the counter to drink it. She was something.

One minute sharp and bitchy, the next sort of soft and sad and awkward. Watching her ask him out on a date was like watching a train derail. Gorgeous women like Anna usually weren't so uncomfortable. Which was the real Anna? Sam wanted to put his money on the soft, sad and awkward girl with the genuine smile and big blue eyes.

"Anna," he said out loud and then shut his mouth. He drained the bottle of water and went back into his spare bedroom where his weights were so he could finish his workout.

A year ago he used the weights to keep his body in shape so he could perform his job and stay on his toes. Now he used the weights as physical therapy so he could regain mobility and just a little bit of the strength he had lost.

It was the only thing he was ever going to get back.

AT 3:00 A.M., Sam was staring up at his ceiling.

Anna. What a piece of work she was. A real piece of work. Sam was fully aware of what he was doing. This obsessing was something he had been battling since the accident. In the deadening never-ending hours of free time, Sam would become fixated on something. Like woodworking. Like long-distance running. Like the stewardess on his flight to Los Angeles last month. Like how, if he had been just a little bit quicker in that hallway, if he had turned right instead of left when the wall came down on him, he wouldn't be where he was now. Anna had joined the list of obsessions.

Let. It. Go. Get some sleep.

But the problem was there was no real reason for him to get to sleep. Nothing to really do in the morning, so he punched up the pillow behind his head and focused some more time and energy on Anna.

"Anna," he said again, kind of liking the sound of her name in his empty room.

"Anna, I don't mind if I do," he said and decided he was going to go on that date with her. He just needed to find out if that woman with the warm smile and genuine eyes existed underneath all the attitude. If she did, if she was there, Sam smiled up at his ceiling... Well, he would find her.

Nice or nasty? He wondered and smiled at all the possible implications. Sam flopped over onto his stomach and shut his eyes, calling up Anna's eyes to fall asleep to. It worked like a charm.

5

DAY THREE of Anna's sabbatical and she didn't think she could take it anymore. So, tired of her own company she agreed to go shopping with Marie for curtains and seat cover material for Marie's new restaurant. Somehow in the course of the day—worn down by gingham and toile, no doubt—she had agreed to go to a restaurant opening party that night with Marie. It was going to be a disaster.

The feeling of dread built while Anna got ready so that by the time she was stomping up the back stairs to Marie's apartment, she was planning how to back out of tonight's opening and vowing to avoid all gingham and toile forever. She knocked hard on the door. After a brief moment, Anna knocked again, getting impatient. If Marie ever opened the door, Anna would tell her to forget it, then convince her to go see a movie or something. Anything other than this... nightmare.

The door finally opened revealing Marie in a gorgeous, form-fitting purple dress that did crazy things to her eyes and boobs. Anna's mood sunk even deeper if that was even possible.

"Forget it," she told her sister. "I am not going." *Why the hell did Marie get all the good genes*, Anna wondered bitterly.

"Well." Marie pushed some black curls off her shoulder and pursed her lips at Anna. "You certainly aren't going looking like that."

Anna looked down at her gray business suit and shrugged. She didn't have "party" clothes. Why would she ever need them? It's not like she went out dancing with Aurora Milan. Anna shuddered at the thought. She had suits, some casual clothes and about four hundred pairs of underwear, that was all. She couldn't even imagine what one was supposed to wear to go out. *Whatever.* She wasn't going, like this or any other way. Marie turned to the side and Anna stormed into her sister's apartment.

"This is a bad idea, Marie." Anna walked into the orange kitchen and, for the first time, didn't cringe. Orange must be growing on her. She opened the refrigerator, looking for a snack. Getting fired and having all this free time had made Anna hungry. She had wondered yesterday after finishing a whole medium pizza on her own, if while working maybe she had never really "eaten." She tried to rack her brain but all she remembered were the occasional Chinese takeout, a lot of salads and fruit shakes. And peanut butter cups. Lots and lots of those.

"I don't know any of these people." She pulled out what looked to be leftover stir-fry. She put the container on the breakfast counter and dug out a fork. "What will we have to talk about? I don't know anything about food or restaurants." She put a carrot in her mouth. "Oh, that's good," she said as the taste registered. Anna looked down at the stuff in the bowl. "What is that?"

"Curry," Marie answered. Anna forked a pepper in her mouth.

"Wow, that is really good."

"You want to heat it up?" Marie asked wryly.

"No." Anna grabbed the bowl and hoisted herself up onto the counter. She kicked off her sensible, black, medium-heeled shoes and settled in to convince her sister to stay home with her and rent movies and eat curry all night long. "Let's not go."

"I have to go," Marie answered, laughing. "Louisa is a good friend and meeting these people will be good for Marie's when I open. And, frankly, you need to go, too. You've been attached by the mouth to my refrigerator for two days. I think it's time you saw some of the outside world."

"I see the outside world," Anna mumbled through a mouthful of chicken.

"Okay—" Marie rolled her eyes "—the world outside of Arsenal and Arsenal clients."

Anna waved her fork in dismissal of that idea. Like it or not, she had very little interest in the outside world. "Come on we'll rent *Pretty Woman* and you can make some dinner and we'll hang out." Anna twisted the screws. "We never just hang out anymore."

Marie took a deep breath and the purple fabric across her chest stretched.

"Careful," Anna warned, "you are going to bust out of that thing." She stabbed a piece of chicken and put it in her mouth, trying, but not very hard, to keep the jealousy out of her voice. Anna's chest had all the topography of Nebraska. Really, she didn't mind that so much, except when Marie flaunted her Colorado skyline all over the place, which frankly, she had been doing since she was sixteen.

This restaurant opening party was a bad idea on a million different levels, not the least of which was that every time she went somewhere with her sister the comparisons would start and Anna always ended up on the losing end. There was every possibility that these comparisons were all in her head, just like Marie had been saying for years, but Anna didn't think so. Besides, what did it matter if Anna was doing the comparing or somebody else? She felt lousy all the same and she just wasn't in the mood for it tonight.

"We can gossip all night, we never gossip." Anna pointed her fork at her sister. "We should gossip more."

"You never have any good stuff." Marie got out a glass and filled it with water. She leaned against sink to drink it. "I supply all the gossip."

"Well." Anna smiled with a certain amount of thrilled delight. "I happen to have some good gossip."

"Let me guess," Marie laughed, clearly scoffing. "You slept until seven o'clock. Or maybe you figured out how to use your oven. Or wait—" she opened her eyes wide "—you..."

"I asked a guy on a date."

Marie blinked. Once. Twice. Her mouth fell open.

"Oh, shut up, it's not that hard to believe." Anna's pride hurt.

"Yes, it is." Marie dumped the water out, reached back into her cupboards and grabbed two wineglasses. "It's a huge deal. This...I can't..." She shook her head and opened her fridge for the bottle of white wine she had there. "Who?" she finally asked.

"A guy named Sam Drynan." Anna took the glass of wine her sister offered. "I saw him without his shirt on."

"How in the world did this happen?"

Anna took her time explaining the situation with Sam Drynan, of the perfect, hairless chest. From her bad behavior in the laundry room to his noncommittal answer to her fake date. When she got to the fake date part Marie groaned and clapped her hands over her face.

"You have got to be kidding me."

"No." Marie's reaction was not what she had been hoping for. Anna knew she didn't handle it well, but she had zero experience in that area and it was Marie's job to tell her it was okay. "But what's the big deal?"

"The whole idea behind asking a person on a date is to make them feel desirable. Fake dates make people feel like tools."

Anna snorted in disagreement, but she knew her sister was right. Of course she was. The few moments of good humor that she had just experienced while she had been bragging about her small triumph in the battle of the sexes van-

ished. Anna was back to feeling like an unemployed, fat—
she put down the curry—useless...

Marie stomped across the tiled floor in her gorgeous, but
very painful-looking, shoes and grabbed Anna's hands.
"Don't you want to take those off?" Anna asked, looking at
Marie's strappy sandals. "Put on some sweatpants..."

"Anna, we are going to this opening tonight. That's final."
Anna started to roll her eyes but Marie gave her a little
shake. "It is not going to kill you."

"Of course it's not going to kill me, but that doesn't mean
it's not going to be torture."

Marie's blue eyes softened for a second and Anna thought
maybe she had her, but her sister shook her head. "I don't
understand why this is so hard for you. I've watched you at
Arsenal functions, why is this so different?"

Anna rested her head back against the cupboards and con-
fessed. "Because there is no goal here," she explained. She
rolled her head over the cupboard enjoying the feeling. She
never noticed how bumpy her head was. Life had been like
that the past few days. Yesterday she'd discovered she could
flip part of her eyelids up. It was weird and gross and she did
it for five minutes in front of a mirror. Sadly, she had that
kind of time on her hands. "I just don't understand what the
point of a party for a restaurant—"

"Fun," Marie supplied. "Companionship. The thrill of
meeting new people."

"See." Anna stopped moving her head and looked at Marie. "That's the difference between us, right there. It's a thrill
for you.

"And torture for you." Marie nodded sympathetically and
Anna could feel the tide changing. She wondered if Marie
had any sweatpants that would fit her and how long it
would take her sister to whip up some more of the curry.
"Well, too bad. We're going." Marie yanked Anna off the
counter. "But you're not going like that."

"Marie..."

"Shut up. There are two kinds of people in this world, Anna." Anna rolled her eyes and mimicked her sister behind her back, mouthing the all too familiar words as they came from Marie's mouth. "People who've got it all and people who know how to use what they've got."

Marie dragged Anna through the hallway to her bedroom in the back of the apartment. Anna followed like she always did. She could not be bothered to count the numbers of times Marie had slapped some makeup on her, changed Anna's clothes and called the results "The New Anna."

A million. Maybe. Since they were very young and Marie discovered lip gloss. Usually "The New Anna" and a happy Marie would just sit around after the makeover, watching *Pretty Woman* and eating chips. Anna hoped that was the way this makeover would go.

The walls of Marie's apartment were lined with photos and posters and art from all the places Marie had visited or lived in her twenty-six years. Shuffling past a weaving from Mexico, Anna wondered if instead of buying crap for her walls she could just borrow some from her sister.

Marie swung her into the bedroom and Anna collapsed onto the unmade bed. Duvet, pillows and bright red sheets slid to the floor and Anna grabbed them and piled them back on Marie's bed.

"When did you paint this room?" Anna asked, appreciating the rich brown walls that somehow made the whole space seem a little more sexy. She should have Marie come over and paint her walls. She could use some sexy. The mouth-drying image of Sam Drynan leaning against his open doorframe without his shirt on popped into her head and she quickly shook it away. Tonight was going to be awkward enough without Sam camping out in her brain.

"Ah—" Marie looked around at her walls for a second "—two days ago, I think. Now, strip," Marie demanded as she started riffling through her closet, firing selections at Anna.

"What's wrong with what I'm wearing?" Anna asked catching something sequined as it sailed past her head. Her gray suit was chic, comfortable and more importantly, it minimized her hips and accentuated her breasts. It was her favorite suit.

"Nothing if you're going to work, but we are going *out*."

"Out," Anna repeated quietly. She held a tiny black leather vest to her chest and fervently wished she hadn't gotten out of bed this morning. She looked at her sister, a wild and gorgeous gypsy who was completely aware of who she was and was confident in that. Anna didn't even want to try to fit into her shoes.

"Come on over here." Marie flipped on the makeup lights around her vanity table. She pawed through her drawers, pulling out tubes of lipstick, compacts and other far more mysterious objects. "Anna?" Marie turned, all black hair, purple dress and devilish blue eyes. She was holding tweezers. Anna put a hand to the eyebrows she knew were soon going to be the object of those tweezers.

"Marie? What exactly are you going to do?"

Marie laughed. "I'm going to pluck the shit out of you."

"YOU HAVE GOT TO BE kidding me," Anna said to her sister's reflection as they looked at the results of Marie's makeup and eyebrow efforts in the bathroom mirror. Marie had insisted on taking Anna's hair out of her perpetual bun and Anna couldn't believe how much hair she had. Long, full and thick, with some wave and it was very pretty. Anna just couldn't believe that it was her hair.

To say nothing of her lips which were red and larger than she had ever seen them. And her eyes—which Marie called "smokey," Anna just called trampy—were definitely bluer and seemed bigger, dominating her small face.

"I look like a hooker!"

"No, you don't!" Marie snapped. "You look like a hot, twenty-eight-year-old woman. Now let's get going, we are already late."

"I am not wearing all of this..." Anna searched for a word that would properly explain how she felt about eyeliner and red lipstick. She usually wore eyeshadow the same color as her skin and the same neutral lipstick she had always worn. What Marie had done to her involved more tubes and compacts than Anna had owned in her entire life. "Gunk, outside."

Marie, who had up until this moment taken all of Anna's bad attitude in stride, turned on her with her eyes lit up with an evil angry light. "We are going," she said through clenched teeth. "You are wearing that lipstick and that shirt," she pointed at the red halter top that Anna was barely wearing. Anna pulled it up and Marie slapped her hands. "You are going to drink anything other than club soda and you are going to talk to every single man in that place if I have to wrestle you to the ground to do it."

Anna considered her reflection again. The red halter top was probably far more conservative on her than it was on her sister, but it still showed a lot of skin. Skin that had not seen the outside world since the early nineties. But still...she looked like a stranger. Standing behind her, Marie cocked her head to the side.

"You look great," she said with a smile that made Anna smile back.

"I look like—"

"A good time," Marie filled in. "You look like a confident and sexy woman who knows how to have a good time." Marie put her hands on Anna's shoulders, tugged the shirt a little lower and grinned wickedly. "Who knows, maybe you'll actually have one."

Anna doubted it, but her eyebrows were plucked and she

had some cleavage. In the three days since she had been fired, she had asked a man on a date and now she was leaving the house in her sister's clothes. She shrugged. "Anything's possible."

TWO HOURS LATER, Anna was really trying to believe that anything was possible. She looked like a different woman, so maybe, for the evening, she was a different woman. This party was a swanky affair and she didn't feel *entirely* out of place. There were women milling about wearing far fewer clothes and, honestly, they didn't look half as good as Anna did. Of course, no one looked as good as Marie, but that was to be expected.

The room was lit up with tasteful white lights and hundreds of flickering tealights on every flat surface. Music of a vaguely dance nature pulsed quietly in the background and Anna watched people moving slightly in time. A woman carrying a tray of little tiny quiche-type things walked by and Anna snagged something that would no doubt taste just as good as the fifty other things she had snacked on since walking in the doors.

Louisa, the owner and chef behind this little soiree, had put together a great party.

So far Anna had not had to talk to anybody. She was a no one in the restaurant biz and she stayed in the shadows. A few men glanced her way. One, a tall fellow with a very nice smile and glasses, kept making eye contact. But mostly she got vague smiles and small nods as people made their way past her.

Marie, however, was the center of attention. She was currently surrounded by four men who were no doubt turning themselves inside out to get her to laugh or toss her hair around or take off her clothes. Anna wasn't bitter. Nope. Not bitter. This suited her just fine.

Anna pulled up her halter top, and checked out the men at

the party. If she looked like a woman on the prowl, she might as well try to play the part. To be honest, she thought most of these chefs were a little short and were all of them nearsighted? Almost every single man had on a pair of funky glasses.

None of them looked like Sam.

She looked down at the drink in her hand. *What do they put in these things?* She wondered. She barely knew the guy and she couldn't shake him from her mind. It was strange and kind of freaky, but the fact remained that this would be a much more interesting time if Sam were here. And he had his shirt off. And he was being a smart-ass. *Much better time*, she thought and took another sip of her drink.

The man who had been making eye contact with her all night, raised his glass to her again and, after as subtly as possible checking that her shirt was still on, she raised her glass back to him. Only to realize it was empty.

"Are you flirting?" Marie asked at her elbow. She replaced Anna's empty martini glass with a full Cosmopolitan. Anna was a new convert to the fruity pleasures of the Cosmo. She didn't even care that Marie called it passé.

"Yes. Yes, I am." Anna took a sip and marveled at how she had ever lived without Cosmopolitans.

Anna Simmons, she thought. *It takes a special kind of woman to be unemployed, drunk and still be on top of the world.* But she was. Flirty guy, with the nice dark hair and the smart glasses, left the group of people he was talking to and started wandering over to where she and Marie were standing. Anna's stomach fell to her feet.

"Get out of here," Anna breathed. "He's coming over." She pushed Marie away with her hip. The last thing she needed was Marie there to distract him. He wasn't Sam, but he was here and she was "The New Anna."

Marie laughed. "You sure you don't want me to stay?"

"Get lost, Marie. Seriously."

"I don't know, he's pretty cute."

"Get..." But it was too late. "Hi!" she said in an overly bright voice as the man came to stop in front of them.

"Hello, ladies," the man said with a gracious smile and Anna felt nothing. Not a single extra beat of her heart. No strange warmth in her stomach. The man, while handsome and right in front of her, left her cold. "I'm Edward." He introduced himself smoothly.

"Hi, Edward," Marie said after an awkward pause. "I'm Marie and this is my sister, Anna."

"Hi, Ed," she said with a stupid, strange little wave. *Ugh.*

"It's Edward," he said with a grin. Anna imagined the floor opening up and eating her.

"Sorry," she grimaced.

"Edward, can I get you a drink?" Marie asked and Anna recognized an escape tactic when she heard one.

"I'm fine, thanks," Edward said still smiling. He was like an Eddie Bauer catalog brought to spectacular life. He was pressed and polished and combed and his smile was engaging without being too engaging. He was terrifying. Sam, or at least the mental image of his scowl and bare chest and the long scar on his back, flashed in her brain and just the thought of him gave her heart a little hiccup.

Suddenly, she didn't want to be alone with Edward. Anna edged closer to her sister in an attempt to get her hands on her to prevent her from leaving. But Marie was quick and gone before Anna could do anything about it.

Hell is small talk, Anna thought.

She took a bracing sip of her Cosmo and hoped for the best.

"So, Anna, are you in the restaurant business?"

"No," she answered, "I'm in advertising. Well...I was."

"You were?" He tilted his head to the side and took a step closer. The music had been turned up and since she didn't want Edward any closer she started to speak loudly.

"I was fired," she said bluntly. "Sort of. What do you do?" she asked, working painfully on her small-talk skills that were not quarterly numbers or slogans or target-audience related.

"I'm a chef. Did you say you were fired?" Edward's eyes were no longer quite so warm, his smile a few degrees cooler.

"Sort of." She shrugged and took a big gulp of her Cosmo. *Let this be a lesson. Do not open the small talk up with "Hi, I'm an unemployed loser."*

"How does one get to be 'sort of' fired?" he asked.

"Well, it's pretty difficult. Apparently it takes years of devotion and hard work," Anna said and laughed. Edward did not. She swallowed. "So, a chef, huh?"

"Over at Lemon and Sage," he said and Anna had no clue what he was talking about.

"So, you're still an employee?" Ed's brow snapped together and Anna tried to remove her foot from her mouth. "I mean it seems like everyone is opening their own place." That wasn't much better, but Anna couldn't stop. "It must be a good tax break." *Oh God, oh God, did I just say tax break? Nothing says sexy lady like tax breaks.*

Edward took a sip of his own drink and almost imperceptibly scanned the crowd over her head. "Yeah," he answered, distracted by something that was going on to the right of her. A little drunk and very perturbed with herself and Ed, Anna turned to see what he was looking at. Marie was posing for a picture with two other men. Marie, of course. He'd probably only wandered over to Anna in order to meet Marie. *Figures.*

"She's gay," Anna lied childishly, but she felt better. A girl could only take so much in a night. Eddie's eyes focused back on her. "You might as well lust after Ellen DeGeneres." His eyebrows snapped together in what was clearly painful disbelief. "She hates men. Hates them. Sorry, Ed." Anna clapped him on the shoulder and left him standing there.

This is a true and painful waste of time, she thought as she drained her glass. She wondered why she bothered. There was no point in this little charade. She was twenty-eight years old, she should know better than to try to be something she definitely was not. And despite prevailing opinion, Anna was okay with what she was.

She found her sister a few minutes later and told her she was going to go home.

"Anna, no," Marie said. "Come on, there will be dancing soon. I'll get you another Cosmo."

"No, I think I've had enough Cosmos. Look, it's late and I've got to get up and..." *Oh God, I don't have to get up for anything. That's depressing.* "Yeah, I'm leaving." She pressed a hasty kiss on Marie's cheek and made her way through the good-looking, small-talking crowd.

She pushed open the door and stepped out into the night. It was cool and the air smelled of jasmine, salt water and red sauce from the Italian restaurant two doors down. Anna took a deep breath and then another. *Better,* she thought. *This is better.* The street was lined with small restaurants and boutiques. People milled about on patios and at street corners.

She could see the skyscrapers of downtown on the horizon and the sight, as it always did, reminded her of where she was and who she was. She had a corner office in one of those buildings. Well, she would in six months. In six months the whole floor would be hers. That's who she was, where she belonged and the sight of the tall buildings against the purple bruised sky made the rest of the tension in her body melt away.

She was very good at what she did. One of the best actually and she just needed to remember that. Some people go through life never feeling good about anything they did.

Anna looked up at the familiar skyline and knew that she had a lot of things to be proud of.

Small talk just wasn't one of them. She considered it for a moment, trading in some of her success for the ability to flirt. Or perhaps the ability to better fill out the red halter top. But she wouldn't do it. Nope.

She was Anna Simmons, advertising executive on her way to the top of the world.

Maybe it was the drinks in her system but Anna decided it was a lovely California evening.

She would walk a few blocks before hailing a cab. She'd had too much to drink and the fresh air would do her good. She got a block down the street before she heard the unmistakable sound of a person in high heels running after her. She stopped and turned to let Marie catch up.

"Anna..." She panted.

"Marie," Anna chastised. "You have people back there who want to talk to you."

Marie looked toward the restaurant for a second, then waved it off. "Pretentious snobs."

"Yeah, but those pretentious snobs are..."

"Not my sister," Marie cut in. She linked her arm through Anna's and they stepped off the curb together to cross the street. "You want to tell me what's going on?"

Anna took a deep breath as they stepped in unison onto the other sidewalk. They strolled past a storefront and all of the mannequins were wearing outfits from Goddess's spring casual wear line. The pink skirt with the little flowers. The white shirt with the crochet inlay, the skirt with the button hem. Anna stopped and looked at the mannequins.

"Marie," she said matter-of-factly. "We are what we are, you know?" She looked at her beloved sister. "I am a woman who loves her job. I am a woman who *is* her job. There's never going to be 'The New Anna.'"

Marie considered one of the mannequins dressed in the

yellow T-shirt and white shorts that Anna had spent a year of blood, sweat and tears marketing. "Don't be so sure of that," Marie said.

Anna laughed and hauled up the halter top that continued to slip down her Nebraska chest. "Sweetheart, it's the one thing I am absolutely sure of."

Marie tugged her back into motion. "Let's go watch *Pretty Woman* and I'll pop some popcorn."

"Finally," Anna said with real relief and Marie laughed, linking her arm through hers. "Do you have any sweatpants I can wear?" Anna asked falling in step with her sister.

Marie laughed again and Anna joined her. Above them the stars came out from behind the clouds. Anna noticed them, admired them and wondered, really, what more was there supposed to be to life. Food, her sister and sweatpants.

Sounded good to her.

6

ANNA GRABBED HER KEYS, looked at herself in a mirror and hoped she was wearing all the right things for a Memorial Day picnic. After spending most of Sunday on Marie's couch with what had to be the worst hangover in the history of the world, she now felt just barely ready to face Camilla and her family. She was wearing jeans, tennis shoes and a T-shirt. Her straight black hair was pulled back in a barrette that she'd found at the bottom of her underwear drawer.

She had been charged with getting Meg's birthday cake. Apparently the dog got into the one Camilla already had. So she had to pick up a cake, fend off a doctor and, most importantly, stop thinking about Sam Drynan.

She had not heard from him so Anna guessed he had thought about her date and decided against it. She couldn't blame him, as first impressions went, she had made an awful one. She knew that. But she had thought, standing on his front stoop, that there had been some sort of small connection between them. It had been a while but those few seconds that they had stood there smiling at each other had seemed special. Different. And more than that, Anna thought that maybe he had thought the same.

Knock it off, she told herself. *You have to get a life and then everything will get back to normal. There is no time to wonder what Sam Drynan is thinking.*

She pulled open the door and there on her small stoop sat Sam. This time with a shirt on. A blue one. Anna's heart, before she could stop it, went *pitter-pat*.

"Hello, Anna," he said, his voice smooth and deep and capable of doing such surprising things to her stomach. He stood up to face her, resting one foot on the step.

"What are you doing here?" she asked.

"You said something about a picnic?" His lips curled a little and Anna looked down at her hands she was so flustered.

"Right." She stepped out onto her stoop and he had to take a step back to keep from colliding with her. "I got the impression you weren't going to take me up on that." The sun was behind him giving him all sorts of halos and she had to squint against the brightness.

"Well—" he shrugged casually "—I got the impression you didn't really want *me* to go. I mean, you were looking for a gay decoy date and there I was."

Jeez, when you put it that way. She nodded. "All right, that's fair."

"Maybe you want to ask me again?" He ducked his head to better see into her eyes.

Anna swallowed hard and felt sweat pop up along her hairline. She turned and shut the door behind her. "You want to go on a picnic?"

"Yep." He grinned and she could suddenly see what Sam looked like as a ten-year-old boy. Cute. Of course.

Anna blinked. "Okay," she said. But she was not about to spend another moment wondering what Sam was thinking. She was too old, too busy for games. She was going to be up front, she *had* been up front. She would expect nothing less from him. She rested her hip on the metal railing and eyed him carefully. "Why?"

He was obviously taken aback for a moment by the bluntness of her question. She crossed her arms over her chest and waited.

"Well." He frowned. "The usual reasons I guess."

"Like…" she prodded, unsatisfied.

"I want to get to know you better."

"That's nice, but doubtful. I haven't been very nice to you," she pointed out.

"Maybe I like women who aren't all that nice," he said with a shrug and Anna couldn't help it, she laughed.

"Well, then I'd say you might need some help."

Sam stared at her with a sort of baffled look on his face and she wondered if maybe the guy really did need help.

"Anna," he finally said and his voice stroked her skin, woke up all the sensitive parts of her body. "I think maybe you're nicer than you think."

Anna was struck dumb.

"We should maybe get going," he said. After a moment— a moment that the thought *I'm getting in over my head. I can feel it already*, flittered through her mind—Anna agreed.

"I'll drive," she said.

THEY STOPPED AT the grocery store around the corner from their condo complex for the cake. She thought the chocolate mousse number was pretty spectacular, but as soon as she mentioned the word "kid," he picked out the giant sheet cake with mountains of white frosting and sprinkles. She couldn't remember the last time she had had a sprinkle.

"What makes you such an expert here?" she asked as they made their way through the parking lot toward her car.

"I've got a big family." Sam shrugged his massive shoulders. "I take it you don't," he asked.

"Don't what?" She had been distracted by his butt. She could barely admit it to herself, but Sam Drynan had a butt that was...well, distracting.

"Have a big family?" Sam said and she could hear the smile in his voice. She sped up, walking ahead of him so as to not be distracted anymore.

"Nope." She rethought that answer after thinking of Camilla and her brood. Particularly Meg. Meg had been born just after Anna got the job at Arsenal and, as a result, she had a soft spot for Camilla's oldest grandchild. "Well, my immediate family is just my sister and I, but my extended family is big. I am sort of an honorary aunt to the little girl whose birthday party we're going to."

"Aunt Anna, that's nice," he said. She turned to look at him, the sun hitting the white gold of his hair and the wild green of his eyes. "I love being an uncle. I assume the same benefits are attached to being an aunt?"

"Depends on what you call benefits," she said. She unlocked the back door and Sam slid the cake onto the seat.

"I don't know, all of the fun none of the tears?"

"Yeah, I like that one," Anna laughed. "I really liked the one that allowed me to give Meg back to her mom for bath time and any sort of diaper changing."

"Yeah, that diaper changing one is at the top of my list, too."

They slid into the car and as they drove out of the parking lot, Anna wondered why this was so easy. This chitchat and easy back and forth, the little exchanges of personal information was usually akin to searching for land mines for her. Tense, unpredictable and sometimes explosive in a bad way. But here she was just talking away with no effort. It made so little sense.

Prince Charming was turning into a nice guy.

GETTING ANNA SIMMONS to crack was taking every bit of energy and charm he had. Sam was getting exhausted just trying to figure out ways to get the closemouthed woman to say anything more than yes or no. Perhaps it was the degree of difficulty that made everything she said that was even moderately personal feel like gold, because everytime she opened up Sam felt like he had won something.

She was a tough one. The women in his experience loved to talk. The right question, or just any kind of question, and they could rattle on for hours. Anna, apparently, was not like other women.

She certainly didn't look like other women. The way the sun came into the windows of her car turned her skin into…well, Sam didn't really know. He didn't have those kinds of words at his disposal. But he just wanted to touch her cheek, see if her skin felt as soft as it looked. She was beautiful, this woman and all of her silences. A beautiful, mysterious woman once he got past all the armor she wore.

"I think you need to be briefed on what you're walking into here," she said. She darted a look at him out of the corner of her bright blue eyes and smiled.

He was breathless for just a moment. *She is something.*

"I'm ready," he said and turned in the seat to watch her more carefully.

"The gorgeous older woman who will be running the show is Camilla Lockhart, my former boss and mentor."

"Former?" he interrupted, which, he could tell by the sudden creases in her forehead, she didn't like.

"Yeah, she's forced me on a sabbatical for six months, but let's not worry about that."

"Wow, six months?"

This time the look she gave him was completely disgruntled. "Yes, but don't worry about it. She's going…"

"What kind of job did you have?"

"Advertising."

That surprised him. People in advertising were usually schmoozers, easy-talkers. She was about as easy as a porcupine. He decided to give the girl a break. "Okay, so what else do I need to know?"

"There's going to be lots of kids."

"I like kids," he said with a smile which, a second later she returned. Sam was no stranger to the vibe this woman was giving him. She was attracted to him, she just didn't know what to do about it.

Perfect, he thought.

"That's great."

"So, do I need to pretend that you and I are in love?" he asked, mostly just to see how she would react. She didn't disappoint, the creamy skin of her neck turned red immediately.

"No, just interested."

"That won't be hard," he said smoothly and watched as the red climbed up her neck and filled her whole face.

Not hard at all, he thought, looking away so she wouldn't see him grin.

"What do you do?" Anna asked after a second. The question, like it always did, had the power to knock the breath right out of him.

Nothing, was on the tip of his tongue. He pulled his sunglasses out of the collar of his shirt and put them on. "I used to be a fireman," he finally said.

"Really?" He didn't look, but she sounded surprised. "Used to?"

"I got hurt."

Anna was no dummy. He knew she would get the hint. He guessed she must have seen the scar that day she came to his place about the decoy date. He hadn't been wearing a shirt so when he had turned to get the address for her, she must have seen it. He watched the scenery pass by and Anna didn't say another word.

CAMILLA'S CAREFUL and calm demeanor was nowhere in sight when Anna and Sam arrived at Lockhart house outside of the city. Camilla lived in a gorgeous two-story, blue, clapboard house with white shutters and window boxes that had some sort of red flower spilling out of them. Camilla and Michael had built the house themselves after Arsenal took off. It was nestled back in some hills and was perfectly secluded and manicured and looked like something out of a magazine.

Camilla, herself, was covered in grass stains, there were leaves in her hair and children were following her around like she had candy in her pockets. Anna was surprised every time she saw this change in her boss. It was as if the woman at Arsenal didn't even exist.

"Hey, you're just in time," Camilla called out when Anna stepped out of the car. "These kids are—" Camilla stopped dead in her tracks and for the briefest moment she was speechless and slack-jawed. Anna turned and saw Sam climbing out of the car in a bright patch of sunlight. He was all smiles and gilding and it was just about as perfect a moment as Anna could have orchestrated.

"Hope you don't mind I brought somebody," Anna chirped just filled to overflowing with satisfaction.

"Yes," Camilla said smoothly, carefully eyeing Sam. "Yes, you did."

"Sam, this is Camilla." Anna made the introductions and as they shook hands she saw Camilla snap back to her old self.

"Sam, it's a pleasure to have you. If you want to follow me with that cake?" Camilla turned and started back to the large two-story house with a trail of kids behind her. Sam brought up the rear.

He shot her a look over his shoulder that was part laughter, part panic and Anna's heart spoke up again with an emphatic *pitter-pat.*

"That's not the fake date guy is it?" Marie sidled up to Anna, her hands filled with plastic food containers.

"Yep, that's Sam. You should see him without his shirt on," Anna answered as they watched him make his way across the lawn.

"You're joking?" Marie breathed.

"No." Anna turned to her sister and clapped her on the shoulder. "No, I am not."

"Annie!" Only one person in the world called Anna Simmons "Annie" and that was Meg.

Meg stood by the garage—one arm in a cast from a rollerblading accident—waving the good one above her head like she was flagging down a high-flying plane. "Hey, Aunt Annie!"

"Hey, Meg!" She took off across the lawn toward the little girl. Meg threw her arms around Anna's waist, pressed her blond head into Anna's stomach and Anna swallowed hard and tried desperately to recall all the billboards and ad campaigns that she had convinced herself were more important than this.

ANNA STOOD in the back corner of the court and prayed that the ball would stay far, far away from her. Camilla and Michael's picnics always turned into some kind of giant sporting event and today was no different even though Meg had injured her wrist, she still got to pick the sport. She picked volleyball and sat on the wide porch steps to cheer while everyone else played in the huge front yard. Anna had tried to avoid getting put on a team, but Meg had insisted and Anna was never very good at resisting the ten-year-old.

"Get ready," Sam mumbled out of the corner of his mouth at her. "I think they've got you pegged as the weak spot."

She glowered at him, but he just grinned back. So far Sam had been doing a very good job of hitting anything that came toward her. And he didn't seem to hold it against her.

"Sam," Michael, Camilla's husband, shouted from his position as server. "Step away from Anna."

"Sorry," Sam joked, shaking his head and inching closer to Anna. "I just can't do it."

Everybody laughed. Michael served and Anna moved out of the way while Sam stepped right in and smacked the ball over the net. He turned back to her and winked before going back to his position.

"Nice one, Annie!" Meg yelled from the patio, where she looked clean and tidy. By comparison, Camilla's other grandkids and all the other children were running around in various stages of disaster. One little boy kept taking off his clothes. One little girl had been found eating grass. Another boy had been sent to one of the upstairs bedrooms for starting fights.

They were animals, all of them. Except for well-behaved, neat Meg. Anna watched her flick grass from her little pink skirt.

She was a gem that one.

"Watch it!" Sam shouted and instinctively Anna put her arms over her head. The ball landed at her feet and bounced.

"That's all right, Annie," Meg yelled from the sidelines.

"No, it's not!" Marie said walking up to Anna. "You gonna pay attention?"

"Yes," Anna lied and rotated with the rest of the players. Meg waved at her, using her whole arm and Anna waved back. Meg clearly didn't care if she paid attention.

Camilla was right across the net from Anna. "My granddaughter adores you," she commented.

"Well, it's pretty mutual," Anna said. Meg's mother Alex, brought Meg a piece of cake and leaned down and kissed Meg on the forehead and Anna's heart clenched painfully at the sweet scene. But, as she always did when that happened, she quickly imagined all the billboards around town hawking Goddess Sportswear.

"Heads up!" Andrew Boyer shouted from behind Camilla who, in one smooth motion, turned and bumped the ball over the net at Anna. Anna managed to get one hand under it and sent it flying behind her. Luckily Marie was there to send the ball back over the net.

"Nice one, sis," Marie mumbled.

"That's not nice, Marie!" Meg shouted.

"Go hang out with the kids!" Marie said and Anna gladly shuffled off to spend some time with her cheerleader.

"Want some cake?" Meg quipped. She held out her plate of half-eaten cake. Anna took a bite of white sugar frosting.

"Careful, if you eat too much your stomach will hurt," Meg advised sagely.

They sat together side by side and Anna ate more frosting. Day five of being unemployed and things were going okay. She was hanging out with Meg, she had a fake date, Camilla seemed to be very pleased...

Her thoughts from the other morning echoed through her head: *get a boyfriend, game over.*

Wait a second...she was on to something here. She put some more frosting in her mouth as the wheels turned in her head. Camilla. Sam. Sam. Camilla. If she could just keep Sam in the picture and somehow make sure Camilla saw that he was, in fact, in the picture, maybe she could get her job back before the six months were up.

The volleyball court erupted in cheers. Her old teammates were high-fiving and hugging—apparently they did much better without her there. The court emptied and people went to find food and drink. Sam, sweaty and laughing, collapsed on the steps at her feet, leaning back so his face was at her knee.

"Want some cake?" Meg asked, and Anna had to smile at her blooming hostess techniques.

"I would love some cake," Sam answered enthusiastically. Meg leaped up, grabbed another paper plate from the table and brought it back to Sam.

"Don't eat too much, it gives you stomachache," she warned him.

"Frosting?" he asked. "No way."

He shoveled all of the frosting in his mouth, getting most of it on his nose and Meg looked at him with childish amazement. "What?" he asked with his mouth full. "What's wrong?"

Meg's and Anna's laughter rang throughout the backyard and Anna happened to catch Camilla's very satisfied smile.

That's it Anna, she congratulated herself. *That's a plan. The proper cooperation from Sam and life as you know it will be back to normal.*

Sam reached past Anna's knee to take the glass of lemonade Meg was handing him. His hand touched her skin and Anna's breath clogged in her throat. If she could just survive the next few months with Sam.

"Watch it!" someone shouted and Anna ducked, but too late. The volleyball hit her in the forehead and bounced up onto the patio where Grant, the five-year-old nudist, grabbed it and ran off into the side yard.

AS FAR AS Sam was concerned, twilight did Anna just right. The blue of her eyes was bluer, her skin even more...what was the word he wanted...pearly? Her skin definitely looked pearly. As they walked across the lawn toward their condo, he could feel the anticipation of touching that skin gather in his stomach.

She had loosened up, she had even laughed a few times. Smiled almost constantly. In the quick and heated briefing he had gotten from Anna's sister, he knew that the laughing and smiling part had not happened in quite some time. Anna, it seemed, had problems relaxing. Well, Sam wasn't one to brag, but he knew how to relax a woman.

"Would you like to come in?" he asked softly, his hands tucked in his pockets. "Have a beer?"

He could practically see the wheels turning in her head. "Yes, I would."

Excellent.

"I have something I would like to discuss with you," she said and Sam's eyes snapped to her face. Something was different here, he could tell. There was a focus to her where there hadn't been one before. Her blue eyes looked at him and they seemed too bright.

"Yeah?" he asked carefully.

"Yes, I have a proposition for you."

Uh-oh, he thought, wishing she meant the kind of proposition he would like, but knowing this was something else entirely.

7

"RUN THAT BY ME AGAIN?" Sam said, shaking his head. The woman had to be kidding. She said proposition, not all-out farce.

Anna sighed and her arm touched his as they sat side by side on the front stoop to his condo. He was confused and flabbergasted, but not so much that he didn't appreciate the zing that traveled along his skin at the contact.

"It's an every-once-in-a-while thing, not all the time."

"You want me to be an on-call boyfriend?" He corrected himself. "An on-call, fake boyfriend."

She pursed her lips at him and that, too, had a pleasant effect on his groin. If he could just ignore the physical attraction, he would have a much easier time telling her to forget it. But the fact was, he was a little riveted. Well, he was plenty riveted. And he wasn't alone, which made things even more exciting. The deep breaths, the sidelong looks, the half smiles, all showed she was plenty riveted herself.

"If that's what you want to call it, yes. I want you to be an on-call boyfriend." She nodded her head and the lights of the condo behind her turned parts of her black hair blue. She took a sip of beer and turned to face him. "I need your help."

Well, shit. Sam swallowed. He had been a firefighter for ten years and requests for help sent things inside of him rallying.

Relax, he told his hyperactive goodwill. *She's not stuck in a tree. She's trying to pull the wool over someone's eyes.*

"What are you planning here?" he asked. He leaned back against the steps so she had to turn to see him. Her leg pressed his and she tried to rearrange herself so they wouldn't touch. She was acting a little bit like an awkward teenager and that turned him on.

Sitting here, the smell of whatever flowery purple bush was right beside the porch and bathed in the yellow light from the house behind him, he felt like...well, he didn't know. He just knew that it had been a while since he had felt this way. Whole. He wanted to put his hands in that blue-black hair of hers, press his face to her neck and just breathe.

Anna told him the story about how her boss put her on forced sabbatical with orders to get a life. In six months, Camilla would retire and the advertising company would be hers.

"Wow, really?" he asked. "President?"

The corner of her mouth lifted. She was clearly proud of this. "President," she confirmed and lifted the bottle to her lips, drinking through her smile.

"Congratulations," he said and touched her arm.

"Thanks. It still takes me by surprise sometimes. I mean, ten years ago it was probably the furthest..." She stopped suddenly. Laughed. Had another sip of beer and shook her head. "Anyway, the point is I like my life the way that it is, so I need to satisfy Camilla for these months..."

"Ah," he said. "Thus the fake part."

"Right, I mean when this is over and my life gets back to normal..."

"There's no time for a boyfriend, on-call or not," he supplied for her.

"Right. So, you understand?"

"Sure, I understand, but it doesn't mean I am going to agree," he told her. He wasn't outraged. He was surprised by her nerve, but he wasn't mad. The way he saw it this was a win-win situation.

"What exactly do you need an on-call, fake boyfriend to do?"

"I'm not entirely sure yet. Picnics, the zoo maybe, some trips to the park." She turned away from him. "The idea is for you and I to run into Camilla and her family. I need to get Camilla's schedule."

He decided it was time the gloves came off to see what Anna Simmons was really made of.

"How fake is this going to be?" he asked. He reached out and touched the skin of her neck where her hair had been swept aside. She whirled, like he imagined she would. He leaned back and watched her, knowing what she could see in his face.

OH, MY GOD, Anna thought. *Oh, dear God.* The skin he had touched was on fire, glowing, warming the rest of her body to unbearable temperatures. The air was thick and soft and she had trouble filling her lungs. She was lost in the shadowed green of his eyes, the curl of his lips. *Oh, yeah,* her body was shouting. *Bring it on!*

"I, ah…" She took a sip of beer. Then another. She drained what was left in her bottle and started to choke. The coughing and hacking broke the mood and Sam leaned up to slap her on the back. "Thanks…thanks…I'm okay," she whispered. Sam was laughing, but the heat and intention in his eyes were still there.

"I'm not very good at pretending I don't feel something," he said and shifted so he was sitting beside her again. He was close—his body, his scent, his breath were all reaching out for her and Anna felt parts of herself reaching right back. "And frankly, neither are you."

Her eyes darted up to his and he just smiled at her. "You're as attracted to me as I am to you," he murmured. He brought up his hand and pushed aside a lock of hair that had fallen across her forehead.

Come on, big daddy! Her body continued its wild screaming. Distracted by the way Sam was leaning into her as if he was going to kiss her, Anna wondered dimly when her body had gotten so crude? And then, suddenly he wasn't just leaning into her. He was kissing her. His lips like clouds against hers. He didn't press further. He just touched his full, perfect lips to hers. Her mind stopped and her body stilled. The moment was in slow motion, time spun out. She could feel every beat of her heart, each small breath she was pulling into her body. She could feel the warmth of Sam around her, through her, heating parts of her body she'd had no idea were cold.

He pulled back for a second and she followed. She brought her hands to his face and pressed her lips harder to his. She could sense that there was something here she wanted. Needed. More than sex. More than desire.

He pulled her body against his. One of them groaned low and the kiss erupted. His tongue touched hers and she ignited. She couldn't get close enough. She ran her hands down the muscles of his back and tried to pull him closer. He pushed his fingers into her hair and held her still while he ravaged her mouth. Lips, teeth and tongue. She gave as good as she got. He bit her lip, she sucked on his tongue.

"Anna," he groaned and she fell back against the steps. He leaned over her, abandoning her lips. He kissed her eyelids, her forehead, her chin. He kissed her neck, then sank his teeth into the soft, sensitive skin there and Anna closed her eyes on a gasp. His hand slid down her side to her breast. He tried to shift, get their bodies closer and the cement steps bit into her back.

"Ouch."

"What?" he groaned, pressing kisses to the skin at her neck.

"Careful, Sam." He tried to sit up and he put his elbow down on her hair, pulling it. "Ouch."

"Sorry," he quickly apologized, pushing himself away. Anna sat up and that was it. The moment was over. They were back to sitting side by side on the porch, but nothing was the same. Things had shifted just enough for her to feel like she was sliding. Or falling. Her body was sending out sparks. Her breath still coming in gasps.

"Wow," he said running his hands through his hair. "I mean…" He looked at her, his lips swollen, his hair mussed and Anna stopped herself from throwing herself into his arms. "Wow."

"Yeah," she whispered. As her mind slowly started to gain control of her body she realized the danger that Sam posed. "This isn't going to work," she said and his head snapped toward her.

"I…" She shook her head. "I have a job to do…. I have to keep my head clear and get this done. It's…" She looked at him, feeling things inside of her body that were once so se-cure and strong break. She felt as if she was a bundle of loose ends. "It's my life."

"Anna." He looked at her carefully. His green eyes stud-ied her face, then her lips, which she knew were just as swol-len as his. He had bitten her, sucked…

"Anna." He touched her hand and smiled ruefully. "It's just sex."

That brought her up short. Just sex. She was twenty-eight years old and this man, who she wanted badly, was offering to be her fake boyfriend *and* have casual sex with her.

Ah, there's the problem. As proven time and time again, Anna was awful at casual. Miserable.

"Just sex, huh?" she asked, tempted.

"Yeah," he breathed along the nape of her neck. Her stom-ach twisted and her nipples tingled and she just about melted onto the cement steps right there.

She wished she could just shrug and finish what they'd started. This was the twenty-first century, it could be just sex. She could do that. Frankly, she would love to do that.

Yes! Let's get naked! Her body clamored.

But she didn't know this man. Didn't know a single thing about him except that he destroyed her focus. She had a job to do and the very dangerous way he affected her mind would not help in getting that job done.

"You know something." She looked at him feeling a little vulnerable. She had no agenda, no plan. She felt exposed. "I would love to have sex with you." Sam grinned and leaned in for what would no doubt be another earth-shaking kiss, but Anna dodged it.

"But it's something I am going to have to think about." She took a deep breath and struggled not to get lost in the beauty and heat in his eyes. *Focus. Focus Anna.* "I have one priority. Get a life and get my job back, that's it. That's all," she said. "I am not about to lose focus now. So, if you want to help me, you have to understand that—" she pointed at the steps "—this may not happen again."

Sam shook his head and looked out in the darkness. Anna hoped that she hadn't lost him as a partner just because she wasn't ready—and might never be ready to jump into bed with him. But if that was what he was looking for, then she had obviously overestimated...

"All right," he said. He stood up, held out a hand and pulled her up. "I'll be your on-call, fake boyfriend. But—" he lifted a finger in warning "—I am planning to sleep with you. I won't do a single thing you don't want me to do." She tried to speak up, since that was a very dangerous proposition because she wanted it all. He put his hands on her arms, his fingers brushing the sensitive skin under the sleeve of her T-shirt. "That you don't *invite* me to do."

Well, she thought, stumped.

"You've got a job to do, I understand that. You need my help, I understand that, too." He dropped her arms and she immediately felt cooler. "I don't want to get married, I don't want a big, time-consuming relationship, either.

"But I want you," he said. "And—" he nodded his head at

the porch where moments ago they had been getting it on like rabbits ''—you want me, too.'' He was about to kiss her again—his eyes were hot and his hands were reaching for her. She took a step back.

A slow, potent smile crossed Sam's face and she wondered why she felt like she had a red flag in her hand and Sam was wearing horns. ''Sam,'' she said with as much cold, hard reason in her voice as she could muster.

''I'll help you,'' he said, ''and I won't do anything that you don't invite. That's the best deal you are going to get.''

She eyed him shrewdly. She wasn't fooled—he was going to try his best to get her to invite all kinds of things. But she was tough. She had a plan. She could handle Sam Drynan.

''Deal.'' She put out her hand and Sam took it, giving it one good, hard shake.

''Deal.''

Sucker, her body shouted.

''RUN THAT BY ME AGAIN?'' Marie asked. She wiped her hair off her forehead leaving a streak of sunny yellow paint across her skin.

Anna sighed and rolled her eyes upward. ''Is that safe?'' she asked looking up at the jumble of wires that were hanging out of the ceiling. They were standing knee-deep in the renovations of Marie's, her sister's new café. What was once a warehouse was soon going to be... Anna looked around at the wreckage. Well, hopes were high that it was going to be a charming little restaurant-marketplace. But the way things looked at the moment, it wasn't going to be anything but a mess any time soon.

''I hope so,'' Marie answered looking up. She turned to find her contractor. ''Jimmy, is that safe?''

''You bet,'' the big man said with barely a glance.

Marie shrugged, rearranged the paint-splattered overalls on her shoulders and went back to painting the old church benches that were going to line the long entranceway of the café. "What's this about making out on the steps?"

"We made out on the steps." Anna stepped over some power tools and sat down on the unpainted edge of the bench and tried not to look smug.

"This was with Sam?" Marie clearly couldn't believe it. Anna was having trouble with it herself. She wasn't the kind of girl who made out with a guy on steps. "Sam, the hot guy from the picnic?"

"Yes." Anna crossed her legs in what she hoped was an adult and confident manner. She even smoothed the hem of the khaki skirt that had been her casual Friday uniform. She felt like a fifteen-year-old. She had woken up this morning and bolted for Marie and some juicy girl-talk.

"Made out how?" Marie asked, obviously still skeptical.

"With our mouths, stupid!"

Marie tilted her head and focused on Anna. "Nope," she finally said. "I just can't see it. You getting dirty on the steps? That's just not the Anna I know."

"Well, too bad," Anna shot back, getting a little pissed.

"So, then what?"

"Then what, what?"

"Did you sleep with him?" Marie bent back down to paint.

"No!" Anna, grateful that Marie couldn't see it, blushed.

"Why not?" Marie asked, as she crouched and continued painting, acting as though they were talking about dry cleaning.

"Because unlike other members of my family I don't engage in casual sex," she said primly. All of her guilty pleasure over her encounter with Sam was vanishing. She fiddled with the edge of her T-shirt. Maybe she should have slept with him. God, it had been so long…

She brought her thumbnail to her mouth and chewed on it delicately.

"You—" Marie pointed her paintbrush at Anna "—don't engage in sex at all."

"I don't know him," Anna said.

"So, get to know him."

Anna cringed. The whole fake dating thing would pretty much forestall that.

Marie stood up and scrutinized Anna. "What did you do?"

Anna tried not to look guilty, tried in fact to continue looking worldly and confident. But Marie was simply too good at seeing through Anna.

"Nothing," she said primly.

"Anna." Marie brandished the paint roller at her. "What did you do?"

Anna tried to explain the agreement and all the sound and logical reasons behind it, but Marie just started groaning, shaking her head in despair.

"A man like that and you're going to ruin it. I should have nabbed him when you weren't looking." She bent back down to continue painting. "I mean God forbid you have a good time. God forbid something happen that's not completely planned three months in advance. God forbid…"

"Sis, as much as I love the running commentary on my life, I know what I am doing." Anna stood up, dodging Marie's angry painting. Yellow paint was speckled all over her sister's face and clothes and it was only getting worse. One should never paint when angry, Anna guessed.

"Camilla's going to see right through this," Marie said.

"No, she won't," Anna disagreed. "Not if you don't say anything."

"I don't know…" Marie drawled and let her sentence dangle with all sorts of threats implied.

Anna blew out a breath and rolled her eyes. "What?" she asked point-blank. Her sister was a master briber. She would extort a saint if she had the goods on him. "What do I have to do?"

"All right." Marie stood up straight and took a step toward Anna. "I promise to not tell Camilla if you promise not to be an idiot to Sam."

"I don't know what you're talking about," Anna tried to lie.

"If something happens between the two of you, promise you'll just let it happen." Anna started to interrupt, but Marie held up her paint roller, stopping her. "You won't explain it away or pretend like nothing happened. Promise me you'll be an adult."

"I am an adult," Anna said, indignant.

Marie shook her head. "You asked me to break up with the one and only boyfriend you ever had. That," she said, "is not adult."

Anna had been twenty-one at the time and Jim would have taken the news much better from Marie, but apparently that was not the point. "Okay, fine, I promise..." Anna trailed off, unsure of what Marie exactly wanted her to promise.

"To just be—" Marie opened her arms wide "—*open* to the idea of Sam."

"Fine, I will be—" Anna mimicked her sister "—*open* to the idea of Sam."

Marie eyed her again, then lifted her hand, spit in it and held it out for Anna to shake.

"Oh, come on," Anna moaned. "We are too old for this...."

"You're never too old for spit swears."

"Well, we're too something. Really, Marie."

Marie just continued to look at her and finally Anna looked around to make sure no one was watching. She spit, as inconspicuously as she could into the palm of her hand and put it in Marie's. Marie laughed and gripped her hand hard.

"All right, all right," Anna said trying to pull her hand out.

"Grab a paintbrush," Marie said once she let go of Anna's hand. "You've got lots of time."

Anna wished she could argue or find something else to do, but there was nothing. She sighed, picked up a paintbrush and started smearing yellow paint on the old church pews.

"So..." Marie said nonchalantly. "About this Sam guy..."

Anna groaned and settled in for the grilling.

"SOFTBALL AT 10 a.m. on Sunday." Anna cradled the phone between her shoulder and ear as she frantically jotted down what Emily, Camilla's assistant and keeper, was telling her. "You're joking?" she replied and grabbed the phone with her hand. "Every Sunday morning?" She shook her head and scribbled down the address Emily gave her. If Camilla and her brood of sports fanatics wanted to play softball and eat hot dogs at the same hot-dog vendor in the park every Sunday, well then, Anna could do it a few times.

There were concerts in the park, baseball games, piano recitals. Michael must be a busy man keeping all of it in order while Camilla ruled the advertising world. Her respect for the very mild-mannered and funny Michael grew ten-fold. It took a special kind of man to let go of the stereotypes and embrace being a house husband.

Camilla was a lucky woman.

"All right, thanks Emily." Anna nodded. "Right, right, I owe you. Dinner for two for a month at Marie's when it opens. Got it." Anna cringed and decided she would wait a little bit longer before telling Marie that news. She hung up the phone and gave into the urge to rub her hands together and laugh.

"I love it when a plan comes together," she murmured and called Sam to reserve her boyfriend for next weekend.

8

"YOU'RE KIDDING ME? You got to be freakin' kidding me."
Johnny Manganello stopped in the middle of the court and
Sam dribbled around him and dunked the basketball.

"The crowd goes wild," Sam joked. He rebounded and
dribbled back to where Johnny was standing, still scowling.
Sam knew attitude was on its way. It always came from John.
"Relax, Johnny."

"You're nuts," Johnny said, his thick mustache barely
moving. His giant belly strained his red sweat-stained
T-shirt and his chest heaved with each breath.

"No, I'm—" John reached out and snagged the ball Sam
was dribbling and held it against his hip with his arm.

"A pretend boyfriend?" John asked, his enormous eyebrows nearly lost in his hairline. He might be the hairiest
person Sam knew. "It's hard enough being a real one. You
getting laid?"

Sam shrugged and tried not to smile. "I don't know yet."

"Stupidest freakin' thing I ever heard."

"It's not stupid." Sam knew that John would never understand, but he gave it a shot. "It's the best situation ever.
Think about it, John. I am a fake, on-call boyfriend and she's
already attracted to me. All of the fun with none of the serious crap."

"So be a real boyfriend."

"Well, she's a bit skittish about that sort of thing."

"Total whack job, just like you," Johnny said shaking
his head.

"Listen, I get to have all of the fun and none of the mess. I don't have to think of the dates. I don't have to pay for the dates. She calls me up and off we go and at the end of the night we make out."

"That's the only part that makes sense."

You have no idea, buddy, Sam thought with serious appreciation for Anna and the time spent on his front step.

"So, you're looking to get laid?" Johnny asked.

Sam thought of all of Anna's armor and the curve of her cheek in the moonlight and the taste of her mouth and decided he couldn't answer that question.

Sam knocked the ball away from Johnny and backed up, dribbling. "Come on. Are we going to play basketball or are we going to talk about women."

"We're not talking about women, we're talking about how you're freakin' crazy." John, however, took the bait and came after him.

He loved playing basketball with Johnny because Johnny played rough. They shoved each other and pushed each other and not ever, not for a single moment, did John back off because of Sam's injury. He would knock Sam down and take the ball and laugh. That was what Sam wanted.

John played basketball with Sam now the exact same way he'd played basketball with Sam before the accident.

"Up yours, buddy," Johnny shouted, stole the ball and shot what Sam had to admit was a very nice lay-up for a man who was five foot eight and weighed two hundred pounds. "You give?" he asked, turning to face Sam. Sam realized the poor man was bright red, his giant belly was heaving with every breath.

Sam could have played for another hour. "Yeah, I give. I brought some water."

Sam walked off to his bag and his old friend limped after him. "Good game, man." John grabbed the water and sprawled back on the grass. Sam bit back a smile as he sat beside his friend.

Sam drank his water and listened to John's breathing return to normal.

"Sam," Johnny started, and Sam almost groaned at the tone in his friend's voice. The serious, we've-known-each-other-a-long-time tone. "When you gonna come by the firehouse?"

Sam didn't answer, instead he lifted his head a fraction of an inch to drink and then went back to staring up at the sky. He knew that it was only a matter of time before Johnny worked up the nerve to start asking these questions.

"The guys, they'd like to see you."

"I see all the guys all the time," Sam hedged.

"Yeah, at people's houses and parties and bars. But you never come to the house. Buddy..."

"I'll come by," Sam said just to get Johnny to shut up.

Johnny chuckled once. "You're lying."

Sam blew out a frustrated breath and sat up. The firehouse. The happiest place in his memory with the best group of men he had ever known. Now that he was no longer part of that group, Johnny wanted him just to walk back in there. Sam shook his head. It was like tearing out his heart. It was too much and, as far as Sam was concerned, he had suffered enough.

He would never go back.

"Another game?" Sam asked standing up. He grabbed the ball and stepped onto the asphalt. He turned to face Johnny, confident that he would not press the issue. It was probably all the man could do just to bring it up. Johnny shook his head and stared at Sam. He tried not to see the sadness or the disappointment in his friend's dark eyes, but it was there.

"You know there's people you could talk about this shit with," Johnny said and Sam almost dropped the ball. "Eddie, when he got hurt, talked to some doctor...a shrink...he said it helped him." Johnny shrugged and stood. "I'm done, man. I'm on call tonight."

Sam nodded, unable to speak past the rock in his chest.

"You be careful with that woman, you'll be pretend married and then you'll really be screwed," Johnny said. He slapped Sam on the shoulder and left. Sam watched him cross the grass and get into his car.

Johnny drove off to the firehouse and Sam looked down at his watch. It was Tuesday; he volunteered at the YMCA, teaching little kids basketball on Mondays, Wednesdays and Fridays. Thursdays he helped a friend who coached a high-school girl's track team, but Tuesdays were usually blank. Mind-numbingly blank.

Sam turned and practiced his free throw for another two hours, until his arms were sore and his shoulders throbbed and he was tired enough that he might be able to sleep. And he might be able to stop thinking about Anna.

ANNA HAD INVITED him over to her house on Wednesday night for some sort of planning deal, although what she could be planning, he had no idea. She might be a little crazy. Hell, Johnny might be right and Sam might be the crazy one. But the memory of that kiss kept popping up in his life. He'd be working out or at the grocery store or watching TV and his hand would suddenly remember exactly what her breast felt like, the smooth curve of her waist. His lips burned with the sensation of her teeth sinking into them.

He'd woken up last night with the smell of her skin in his head. The sound of her rare laugh in his ears. It was crazy. And fantastic. The idea that he would get to see her more and slowly work on those spectacular defenses she had built up around herself filled him with that feeling...that... Well, he didn't really know the words for that feeling, but he was excited. It made him want to laugh for no good reason.

He couldn't remember the last time he didn't know what a

woman was going to do. He had kept his relationships with
women casual and friendly—some very friendly—but never
had he been as surprised by someone as he was by Anna.

He knocked on her door and it opened a little as it wasn't
completely shut or locked.

That's not smart, he thought. A woman on her own leaving
her door unlocked. He would have to have a little talk with
her about that.

"Hello?" he called out, pushing the door open a bit. He
was early, having got bored waiting for the right time to roll
around. Maybe she wasn't ready. Maybe she was showering
or walking around naked.

He pushed the door open more. "Hello?"

"Come in!" she shouted. He stepped into her condo. It was
the exact same layout as his. Small foyer, open concept living
room-dining room. A kitchen he couldn't see and the hallway in front of him led back to bedrooms and a bathroom.
The house smelled as though she had spilled bleach somewhere.

Anna came out from the kitchen.

Sam's heart stopped for a second, then started again in a
hard, heavy rhythm. She was a thin woman. Tall and lithe
like a long-distance runner or a dancer. Wearing a pair of
shorts and a T-shirt, she made his mouth go dry.

"Hey, Sam," she said brightly.

"Hey, Anna."

"Come on in. Can I get you a beer?"

He nodded and she disappeared back into the kitchen.
Sam made his way through her place and realized that every
wall was completely bare. And white. As though she had
just moved in.

"How long have you lived here?" he asked. He was no
decorator, but even he managed to paint a wall or two and
put posters up.

"About six years," she answered coming back into the

room. She handed him a beer and even though he tried, he couldn't manage to get their fingers to brush. *Damn,* he thought, *losing my touch.*

"Six years, huh?" He looked around. "I love what you've done with the place."

Anna surprised him by laughing. He had kind of expected her to get a little prissy with him for his joke. "Yeah, I'm a regular Martha Stewart," she said and sat down at the table. She had her own beer and she took a sip as she looked around at her bare walls. "The truth is I never really had the time to do anything with the place."

"Workaholic?" he asked, pulling out a chair across from her.

"You could say that," she answered wryly. She bent her knee and put the heel of her foot on her chair and even that was sexy to him. The curve of her leg, the faint sheen to her skin.

"I can relate," he said before he could stop himself. He took a sip of beer before any more little tidbits from his own ruined life could fall out of his mouth. *Jeez, put a girl in shorts in front of me and I lose it.*

"So, what have we got here?" he asked looking around at the table piled with paper and markers, instead of meeting her eyes. He wanted to avoid any questions she might have about him and his life. It might not be entirely fair, but he was just a fake date, the regular rules about dating and exchanging private information in equal parts did not apply.

He noticed her laptop was open and connected to a projector that was pointed toward one of her blank walls.

She is nuts. He looked up to see if she was serious about all of this and was momentarily lost in the picture she made. She was focused on the screen in front of her and her lower lip, which he knew to be soft and full and perfect, was caught under her teeth.

Her hair was up in a sloppy bun and her neck was right

there for the world to see. *That neck...* Another one of those sensory memories hit him and he remembered how fine her skin felt under his fingers, how soft it was under his lips.

She put on a pair of small glasses and he barely managed to suppress a groan.

That's what this is all about, he thought trying hard to make the ground beneath him solid again. It was one thing to take on a distraction, but the way he felt was quickly growing out of control. And looking at Anna he realized what it was.

Anna was the naughty librarian fantasy. The glasses, the hair, the prim tilt of her nose, all of those defenses covered up a sex-crazed woman. And he knew it, too. A few minutes longer on his porch the other night and she would have been naked and...

"Walkie-talkies and some binoculars." Anna had been talking and Sam finally focused in.

"Whoa, whoa. What are you talking about?"

She looked up blinking her big blue eyes at him. "Equipment."

"For what?"

"Sam?" She shook her head at him. "Pay attention." She pushed a stack of papers toward him. "If you want to start there, we'll go through this step by step."

He turned the set of papers around so he could read the print: Mission Statement.

He laughed. "Are you joking?" he asked and looked up at her very serious face. "I guess not."

He sighed and fell back into his chair. He was in way deeper than the thought.

ANNA FELT GOOD. She felt very, very good. The situation was in her control. She had spent the past two days working on her plans, creating the presentation, ironing out wrinkles. It felt so good to slip back into the vernacular, into the effort it took to put together a plan. The jumble of loose ends in the pit of her stomach were no longer loose.

Instead, she felt a little feverish. As if her whole body was just a few degrees warmer than normal. Having Sam in her condo was not exactly cooling her off. The man was...amazing, Anna had to admit.

She was ready to blame the fever on her suddenly over-wrought sex drive. The almost five-year hibernation of her libido was making her...well, for lack of a better word, hungry. And Sam was looking like dinner.

Though he may look good, she had the sinking suspicion that he wasn't taking her plan too seriously. She would change that. Her PowerPoint presentations had certainly made believers out of tougher nuts than Sam Drynan.

"Let's get started." She clapped her hands together, then turned off the lights. The first screen of her presentation flashed on the bare wall of her living room.

"I have sketched out a plan for the next few weeks in regards to the project...."

"What project?" Sam asked.

"Getting my job back."

"You're calling it a project?"

"What would you call it?"

"Getting your job back," he said, deadpan.

"Well," she drawled, "you can call it whatever you want. I'm going to call it a project."

He shrugged and went back to the papers he had propped up on his legs. He took a sip of beer and Anna got herself back on track. *Time line, right.* "I've looked at the numbers and have created what should be a very feasible time line for the project." She put a little emphasis on the word project. He chuckled and shook his head but didn't say anything. "If we can consistently 'run' into Camilla at least once a week, I believe that I will—" she brought up her hands for the quotes gesture "—have a life, in no less than three months.

Hopefully resulting in my getting back to Arsenal well before the six-month deadline."

Sam was silently staring at her, which she took as a good sign. "Of course, we don't want to be too obvious. If we can up the meetings to two times a week in the later weeks, I believe my chances of getting back to work before Thanksgiving improve by roughly 42%."

"Give or take?" Sam asked dryly.

"Exactly." This was going even better than she thought. "Of course, if we went with an idea I had last night that we announce our engagement…"

Sam splattered the table with the beer he had been in the process of drinking.

"Fake, of course," she told his wide-eyed, pale face. "But I decided against it—the returns just didn't warrant that kind of aggressive move."

"Thank God," he breathed and mopped up the table with his copy of the mission statement.

She flipped to the next screen—Objectives. She started to talk, but clearly Sam wasn't paying attention—he was laughing too hard to hear her.

"This isn't a joke, is it? You are completely serious, aren't you?" he asked, obviously not appreciating her PowerPoint presentation.

"Of course I'm serious," she said primly. Perhaps she had gotten carried away here, but, well, this was the kind of stuff she did. "Look, if this is going to work, we have to be on the same page."

"Okay." He leaned forward and put his copy of the game plan on the table. "Tell me why you don't just ask for your job back."

"You think I *didn't* do that already?"

"All right, so why do we have to plan all this stuff out?" he asked. He lifted the pages and scanned some of them. "I get it that you want us to run into her in different places and that's fine. We can do that." He stopped at one page and held it up to show to her. "But do we need charts? I mean really?" He flipped to another sheet and held it up. "And diagrams?" He looked at said diagram and laughed more. "Softball diagrams. I think I can handle this."

She took a deep breath, prepared to let him know in no uncertain terms that his attitude here was unappreciated. These sorts of precautions were what separated failed projects from successful ones and she needed to be successful.

"It doesn't hurt to be pre—"

"Have you ever played softball?" In the dim light Sam tilted his head and his eyes seemed to look all the way through her.

"No," she answered truthfully. "I haven't." She restacked her papers and set them at right angles on the table in front of him. Anything not to look directly into those eyes. "At Camilla's family picnics I have become an invaluable umpire."

"Ah, sweetheart," he said. Anna's heart stopped, her skin evaporated and she became a puddle of goo over the endearment from this handsome hunk of a man. "I'll teach you."

I bet you will! Her body purred.

Anna looked squarely at Sam, forcing herself not to dump everything off the table and lay him out like a buffet. "Okay, I agree that I might have overdone—"

Sam chortled and she talked over him. "But this is important to me."

"What happens if you don't get a life or whatever it is that Camilla wants from you?" he asked.

"I'm fired for real." The breath she took shuddered in her chest and she knew that she was revealing too much, but she couldn't seem to stop herself. "This is my life, Sam. I love my job. I mean, to not be able to do it anymore..." She was suddenly at a loss for words. He was watching her so intently that she wanted to let it all spill out, every sad and bad decision made to land her in this desperate spot. "It would just kill me." She shook her head and fluttered the edge of her stack of papers with her thumb, waiting for him to laugh at her.

"Well, then—" he put down his beer and picked up his mission statement "—on with the slide show," he said, his voice a little huskier than before. Anna remembered the scar on his back, the fact that he used to be a firefighter. Perhaps he understood what this meant to her, perhaps he was...

"Sam?"

"What?" he asked not looking at her.

"Did you like your job?" she asked. The silence seemed thick between them, as though it had a special dimension keeping them so separate. Far more separate than just the few feet between them. She thought he wasn't going to answer and was about to tell him to never mind when he finally cleared his throat.

"Yeah, I loved my job."

"How long were you..." she trailed off, looking down at her hands and then back up at him. His eyes did not move from the papers on his legs. She watched his throat move.

"Fifteen years. Volunteer all through college and then I joined the department when I graduated."

"Do you miss it?" she whispered, feeling small in all the tension.

"Every minute." He finished his beer.

"What happ—"

"Let's not talk about it, Anna," he interrupted quietly, obviously knowing where she was going to go with her questions. He didn't look at her, but she could see the muscle in his jaw bunch up, and the tension in him was palpable. Anna said nothing. Sam wanted his privacy she could appreciate that.

But the unasked questions burned in the back of her throat.

What happened to you, Sam?

One hour and two beers later, they were done. Sam had fallen asleep for a moment during the budget part of the plan. He laughed when she got to the part about public displays of affection.

"Holding hands and kisses on the cheek?" he asked.

"Or the forehead," Anna pointed out past the lump in her throat. Sam's eyes were easily the most expressive things she had ever seen. Just the mention of the word kiss and they heated up and she could tell he was thinking of all her places he had already kissed. And when she looked at him, she could *feel* all those places he had kissed. Like those glow-in-the-dark stars Meg had up in her bedroom, Anna was sure her neck, her lips and the tops of her breasts were glowing in the dark room.

"And in private?" he asked.

"We will have to…ah—" she swallowed "—wait and see." She quickly scanned ahead to dates she wanted to reserve with him.

But in the end, he had been mostly polite and asked regular questions. When Anna turned the lights back on, he stood up and stretched in the doorframe between the living room and the small bathroom. He was a tall man and, with his arms overhead, he could press the palms of his hands on the top of the frame. He bowed forward, the bottom of his shirt lifted and she could see a small slice of skin. Tan and muscled with just a little bit of hair.

Anna busied herself putting things away.

"You hungry?" he asked. Anna's head snapped back toward him. "I'm starving. Let's go get a burrito."

Anna was starving, too. She would have loved to get a burrito. She looked at Sam, at the skin of his stomach and felt nervous and unsure. She looked down at the stacks of work she had done, work she could stretch into the night if she wanted to, and felt strong and focused.

She forced herself to meet Sam's eyes and lied.

"No thanks, Sam. I'm not hungry." The moment stretched and she almost caved, she almost lost her way.

"Okay," he said and, as he walked by her, he pressed a tender kiss to her forehead. Her eyelids shut and her breath clogged. He pulled away, then walked out her front door.

"You're such an idiot," she whispered into the cool, darkness of her lonely apartment.

9

THE TINY WALKIE-TALKIE in Sam's hand buzzed to life and Anna's voice, disembodied and crackly, came out of the device.

"Sam, can you hear me?"

"Ten-four, good buddy," he said in his best Burt Reynolds accent. Or was it Kris Kristofferson? Whichever, it was the voice every little boy used when talking into a walkie-talkie. Anna might be nuts, but the walkie-talkies had been pure genius.

"Sam," she said and the laughter in her voice was clear even through the small speaker. "Do you see them?"

"Nope," he answered quickly. He disengaged the button and ordered a hot dog from the concession stand.

"Are you looking?" Her voice crackled.

"Absolutely," he lied and paid the guy behind the counter and went to get some mustard. One could not have a dog at a baseball game without mustard. *Naked dog.* Sam nearly shuddered to think about it.

"Sam..."

"Yeah, I'm not really looking. You want a hot dog?" They were at a Giants game on one of those rare, perfect days. Pacific Bell Park was notorious for its wind and fog, but not today. Sunshine and cool breezes all the way. He wanted to skip his duties as fake boyfriend, grab some beers and Anna, then just sit in the bleachers to catch fly balls and occasionally try to look down the tank top she was wearing.

But Anna had been able to narrow down the location of

the Lockharts' seats to one eighth of the stadium. Anna was standing at one tunnel and Sam was at another with roughly one thousand people between them. He was supposed to be looking for Camilla and her family so he could "accidentally" bump into them and get invited to sit with them. Then he was to excuse himself, get Anna on the walkie-talkie and tell her his coordinates before going back to sit with Camilla's brood. Once Anna arrived, he was to act as though he was infatuated.

The only thing remotely simple about the plan was that last part. Sam had to admit, Anna was infatuating. More and more, almost by the minute. He had been surprised by her refusal to go get dinner the other night—he had been sure she would go. But, it seemed, this particular tough nut was going to need a little more work.

"Sam, hot dogs aren't part of the plan." Anna's voice buzzed him out of his thoughts.

"Hot dogs are an important part of any plan." He waited for it, waited and there it was, her laugh over the walkie-talkie. Got him every time.

He was feeling a little giddy. He hadn't been to a game since he was a kid, but the smell of the hot dogs and popcorn, the people around him shouting and laughing, the slices of blue sky and lovely perfect green grass that he could see through the tunnels, all combined to make him feel ten years old again.

"I don't see them," he said as he looked around at the crowd of people cruising by him. He dodged some kids who raced around followed by harried-looking fathers. There were lots of old men wearing plaid, but no stunning silver-haired women. "Let's go sit in the bleachers and have some beers," he suggested, unwrapping his hot dog and taking a giant bite.

He was looking forward to the day. This morning she had brought him coffee and she was wearing shorts again. She even let him drive. The conversation between them had been comfortable and every once in a while she laughed.

Suddenly, a lovely, silver-haired woman was standing in front of him. She was familiar even without the pack of children surrounding her.

"Sam?" she asked with a smile. "It's Sam, right?"

He swallowed and tried very hard to put the walkie-talkie in his pants pocket without letting her see it. "Sam?" The walkie-talkie crackled and buzzed in his hand and Camilla looked at him in confusion.

"Hello, Camilla," he said loudly. "What a—" he laughed a little, he couldn't help it "—surprise."

"You a baseball fan?" she asked.

"I am. I am a huge baseball fan." He couldn't believe it, but he was nervous. He felt like he did in elementary school when Miss Blakely caught him with a pocketful of firecrackers. He had never been a good liar—he should have remembered that. He felt the tips of his ears glowing red. "Huge."

"Sam?" It was Anna behind him. *Oh, thank God.* "Why did you turn off the...? Camilla." In the panic of the moment, he put an arm around Anna and hauled her up against his side.

"Look who I found," he said with a laugh that sounded fake even to him.

"Camilla, what a surprise," Anna said. To Sam's horror, she sounded even worse than he did.

Camilla looked at them skeptically and Sam could hardly blame her. They were acting like idiots. "You guys are here...together?" she asked.

"Sure thing," Sam said, loud and fast as if that might help. He hugged Anna a little closer, then realized he was squishing her and dripping mustard down her arm. There was some panicky laughing while he fumbled around with his napkin and her arm.

"Yep, we're together." Anna grabbed the napkins out of his hands and threw them in the garbage, then awkwardly patted him on his chest. He went to put his arm around her and she ducked at the wrong time and he got her in the nose with his elbow.

"Ouch."

"Sorry."

Suddenly, Camilla's smile broke wide-open. "Well, that's wonderful. Why don't you guys come join us? We've got box seats behind home plate," she said.

Anna and Sam looked at each other for a moment and he could read all of the same lucky amazement that he felt in her face. The crazy harebrained plan actually worked.

They turned to face Camilla. "We'd love to," they said in unison. Camilla led the way through the dark tunnel. When they hit the bright sunshine, the grass and sky and the white lines on the field looked like something imagined. Sam grabbed Anna's hand and squeezed it.

She squeezed his hand back.

Oh, he thought, *this tough nut is cracking*.

ANNA WAS SLIGHTLY SICK. The last hot dog had been one dog too many. She would have to remember that three were her limit.

"That worked out pretty well," Sam drawled from behind her as they walked up the sidewalk to her condo. "I mean, despite the fact that Meg threw up on my shoes, you got hit in the head by a foul ball and we are both terrible liars, I think it went pretty well."

Anna laughed. Put that way, the day had been a dismal failure. But in all honesty the day had been great. Fun. A lot of fun. She couldn't remember the last time she had had that kind of fun.

"You are a terrible liar, I am an average liar. There's a big difference."

Her nose was sunburned and her whole body was electrified by the hours spent in Sam's proximity. He was such a casually demonstrative person. The whole damn day his hands had never left her body for longer than a few minutes. Brushing her shoulder, stroking her hair or her arms, kissing her cheeks and forehead. After hours of that she was so turned on she could barely stand her own skin.

He had lit a slow burning fire inside of her and she didn't know what to do. Which way to turn. She had been telling herself on the way home that she really didn't know this man. He never said a single thing about his life.

Before she had realized it, she had Jim's whole history before she slept with him. She knew his family medical history, how much money he made, how many women he had had sex with and whether he cheated on his taxes.

She knew Sam used to be a firefighter and that he was hurt and that he had some sort of sick love affair with baseball stadium hot dogs. It wasn't enough. Not nearly enough to make the plunge into being his lover. She felt too vulnerable. Too...uninformed. And uninformed decisions were bad ones. Everyone knew that.

She took the steps up to her door, two at a time, put her key in the lock and started to turn to face Sam. To tell him good-night, to steel herself for what would be a devastating kiss. But before she could turn he was behind her. He put his foot carefully between hers and his hands came up to the door by her head. She was caught, trapped and the fire in her raged hotter.

"Anna," he breathed onto her neck and her own breath shuddered in her body. Just like that she went from fully functional human to mindless, boneless, hormone-driven woman. "Anna," he breathed again and kissed her neck. He found the sweet spot just behind her ear and laved it with his tongue. She could feel it in her toes. She let out a slow breath and tilted her head so he could do his worst to her and he did. He opened his mouth and gently bit her neck. He bit that sweet spot and Anna gasped, jerked as though she had been electrocuted. He did it again.

The moan was hers. She leaned back against him. He sucked the skin he had just abused into his mouth and one hand slid from the door to her arm, her waist and finally— *oh, yes*—his hand cupped her breast. When he found her nipple already hard, he chuckled, stirring the sensitive hair on the nape of her neck. He palmed her, squeezing and pinching skin that was already sensitive beyond bearing. He was growing rough and she was shocked to realize that she loved it. Needed it.

"Anna," he breathed again.

Yes, yes, come on, do it! "More," she panted. What she wanted more of she wasn't entirely sure, but Sam seemed to know. His hands became rougher, the words he murmured in her ear more vulgar, his breath faster.

His teeth grazed her ear and his knee came up hard and hot behind her. He had her on her toes, her hands braced against the door.

"Oh, Sam," she groaned. She tilted her head back searching for his mouth and he gave it to her hot and wet and as demanding as his body. She reached her hand around his head and pulled on his hair, suddenly desperate to be closer, desperate to have him.

"Anna." His hands rushed over her breasts to hips and back again. He dragged her higher up on his body and she could feel his erection against her bottom. They pressed hard against each other. "Anna, let me in," he said roughly into her ear. He bit her again and she moaned. He pushed her flat against the door, his mouth at her ear. "Anna, open the door," he breathed. "I've got to touch you."

She fumbled for the key, tried to turn it to let him in, but his hands were still sliding over her body. He palmed her breast, rolled her nipple and her knees buckled. He chuckled knowingly in her ear and that hand slid slowly down her body past the waistband of her shorts.

"Or maybe..." His fingers traced the outside center seam past the zipper right to the hot, wet center of her. "Maybe you want me to do this right here?" he asked, teasing and naughty.

No one had ever talked dirty to Anna and she had no idea that she would respond the way she did. He pressed his erection against her again and she knew that this was barbaric, yet nothing had ever turned her on more. "Anna?" he asked, his finger tracing the seam, pushing hard against her clitoris through her clothes. "Anna." He kissed her neck, his tone calm. She turned in his arms, her eyes locked with his in a moment of silent and desperate need before she buried herself in his lips, unable to get close enough. Unable to touch him enough. His erection was hard and tight against her. She pushed her hips toward him and he groaned, bending forward at the waist. "You're killing me, Anna. Open the door or, I'm not kidding, it will be right here."

She fumbled behind her for the door again and he leaned down to her breast, taking the nipple in his mouth through the cotton of her T-shirt. She cried out and grabbed at him for balance, the door forgotten again.

Suddenly, directly in front of them in the parking lot a car started and the lights tore into the cocoon of darkness that hid them. They leaped apart in the bright, white light like the guilty teenagers they had turned into. Anna saw Sam squint into the light, but she just turned away, pressing her hands to her eyes.

What had she almost done? And on the porch, too. That's twice. The man had some kind of secret power or something.

The car pulled out of the parking space and the lights cut away from them, illuminating a row of trees and the porch. The car honked and someone laughed. "Don't let us stop you," a man yelled. Anna really just wanted to die. Just wanted to melt right into the earth.

From behind her Sam started to laugh, a deep rumble that Anna felt in her chest as much as heard. He wasn't even touching her and she could still feel him on her skin. Inside of her skin. He continued to laugh and finally she had to smile, then she chuckled. Then they were both laughing like two loons, leaning against the railing as they caught their breath.

"Come on, Anna," Sam said compatibly. "Let's go inside before the neighbors start complaining." He stood and touched her elbow and she jerked at the contact. Jerked away from him.

She looked up at him and saw the slow demise of his humor. Finally, he just closed his eyes and swore. "Are you serious?" he asked. She knew he was trying to keep the edge out of his voice, but it was there. "Three seconds ago you were going to screw me against your door and now you're saying no?"

"Yes," she said, unsteady. "Yes, I am saying no."

Her heart beat hard as he watched her. He could push her, just a little. One of those half smiles and she would go back to screwing him against the door.

"Why?" he asked. "I mean, I get it that it's your prerogative, I respect that. But you're not a game player, so you've got to have some reason. I think I deserve to know why."

He did. It was true.

"And none of your garbage about not having room in your life for sex, because we both know that's crap." He gestured to the door, the scene of the crime. That, too, was true.

"Because I don't sleep with strangers," she whispered into the cool air between them.

"We're hardly strangers," he scoffed.

"What do I know about you, Sam?" she asked. All her sexual frustration morphed into something new. Something jagged and she aimed it at Sam. "You know everything about me and I know nothing about you. Nothing."

"Okay, what do you want to know?" he demanded roughly in what was not at all inviting to personal conversation.

"That's not fair," she cried.

"Yeah, well, neither is this," he bit out, but Anna didn't care.

"All right." She took his bait knowing this wasn't going to go well, but unable to stop it. "You were a firefighter, and you were hurt. That's the scar on your back, right? You were hurt in a fire."

"Yes," he answered tightly. Obviously he didn't want to talk about it and she was torn between understanding why he wanted privacy and being upset that he could share such a devastating passion with her but not a single detail about his life.

"When? How? What...?"

"Anna," he interrupted in a strangled voice. His face was white in the darkness and the tension in him almost broke her heart. *Dammit, he started this.* But she didn't have the power to go through with it.

"I'm sorry," she breathed. She reached out a hand but stopped herself, let it drop back to her side in a sort of surrender that she didn't understand. "But, I..." She swallowed. "I don't sleep with strangers. And Sam, you are very much a stranger to me. It's obvious..." Why did this hurt? What was this pain in her stomach, her chest? "It's obvious that that's okay with you. Being strangers..." she trailed off, feeling stupidly like she was going to cry.

"What do I know about you, Anna?" he asked tightly. Her eyes leaped to his and she saw something she had never seen before. He was a cornered man and she braced herself for whatever he might do. "You're a workaholic with no family and no friends. You have to pretend to have a life because you've never known what it was like to have one." He took a step toward her and she held her ground, though she felt things inside of herself breaking. "You want me so bad, but you can't make me fit into your dull and sterile life so you're pushing me out. Well, I get it, Anna. I get it and I'm gone."

Sam turned and walked away.

THE PHONE WAS RINGING. Anna lifted her head from the pile of pillows she was buried under and blinked into the bright morning sunshine that was coming into her room. All that sunlight hitting the white walls and her white sheets nearly blinded her.

She looked around for her alarm clock feeling like a mole emerging from a hole.

Nine o'clock. Jeez. Anna's deeply repressed laziness was taking over. She had the crystal clear memory of her mother sleeping on the couch while Anna and Marie tiptoed around her until the early afternoon. That was almost every morning. Every day. A few more months of unemployment and Anna would be doing the same. Before she knew it she was going to be packing everything she owned into her car and freeloading off the little bit of family she had.

The phone rang again and she fumbled around on her bedside table to answer it hoping, before she could stop herself, that it might be Sam and that he might be as sorry as she was.

Stop it, she told herself. *Stop doing this.* She had been doing nothing but think about Sam since he walked away from her last night. It was ridiculous.

"Hmm?" She croaked into the phone.

"Anna?" It was Camilla and Anna's eyes snapped open. "How are you?"

"Wonderful," Anna said. She cleared her throat of sleep and rubbed her eyes. "I just got done planting a garden," she lied. "You'll have to come over and see it."

"Very funny," Camilla chuckled. "I was calling to see if you had any plans for the afternoon."

Anna thought about it for all of three seconds. She could lay in her bed all day long and think about Sam and her dull and sterile life. "No, I've got no plans," she told Camilla. "Unless you want to make pottery or do that dumb Tai Chi thing, then I'm very busy."

"My daughter Alex and I had an afternoon booked at the Red Door Spa and she can't go. Are you interested?"

Spa, huh? She had never been to one. She had had massages and the occasional pedicure with her sister, but a whole afternoon at the spa? Never.

"What's that entail?" she asked, skeptically. She had heard that they did strange things with seaweed and mud.

"You'll love it, I promise. Now, are you in?"

"Sure." Anna shrugged. "I've got nothing else to do."

"No," Camilla agreed with a laugh. "No, you don't."

WHILE ANNA WAITED on the patio of the designated coffeehouse for Camilla, she sipped her espresso and contemplated her "sabbatical gift" from Marie. A pair of yellow flip-flops. They used to have flowers on them but Anna tore them off, telling Marie that really, it was enough that she was wearing flip-flops, they didn't need to be flowered. But as she looked at her feet and the yellow flip-flops, Anna made the realization that flip-flops were, in fact, the perfect footwear. Comfortable, breezy, there was no foot odor issue and the foam was just high enough to give her skinny legs a little bit of glamour. Not to mention the fact that every single person was wearing them. It seemed flip-flops had taken over the world when Anna wasn't paying any attention.

She was twenty-eight years old and had never known what she was missing.

She sighed, crossed her feet at the ankles and slouched in her aluminum chair as she watched the world go by on the

other side of the patio fence. What were all these people doing? The sidewalk was packed with men and women who
weren't at work. Anna checked her watch. It was 11:00 on a
Wednesday morning. *Don't these people have jobs?* she wondered.

Anna smiled at the server as she dropped off the steaming
cinnamon roll. Anna recognized the girl from the few morn-
ings she had had coffee here. She had gotten so tired of sleeping and counting her socks and going shopping with Marie
and thinking of excuses not to go shopping with Marie that
she had finally sought refuge at this coffee shop on the corner.

That had been a week ago and now she was something of
a regular.

It had become a completely new experience. Not the coffee
so much as the event of it. *Going* for coffee and sitting around
to read and eat pastry was pretty novel. But, much like dis-
covering that the cinnamon rolls she had been eating almost
every morning from this very coffeehouse were a million
times better warm, it was a real pleasure.

Being unemployed did have this one benefit.

Anna bit into the roll and wondered if maybe all those
people on the other side of the patio fence were all servers at
the hundreds of restaurants in the city. Because there was no
way there could be that many unemployed or independently
wealthy people on the streets of San Francisco at 11:00 on a
Wednesday. *Could there?*

Perhaps they were all unemployed and injured firefight-
ers? Her stomach clenched and her heart tripped hard in her
chest. She couldn't think of the man without the sharp pain
in her stomach. She wished she could regret having stopped
the events of the other night, but that was as futile as wishing
there could be a new Anna. She was who she was and she
couldn't help it if she was cautious. She couldn't help it that

she was the exact opposite of casual. Just as much as she couldn't help missing Sam.

Which, she tried to tell herself, was ridiculous. *You can't miss a man you don't know. You can't miss a man who thinks you are sterile and dull,* she thought. The pain in her stomach bloomed in her chest. That had hurt. It still hurt.

She *was* sterile and dull and having him around had made her...she shook her head. She had to stop this. She had already been through it all. Ad nauseam.

She was who she was. Anna Simmons. And he, as he had told her, was gone.

But, even though she knew it was dumb, she missed him. She missed him very much.

The patio was bright and sunny and Anna pulled up the hem of her skirt a fraction of an inch thinking perhaps she might tan her outrageously white skin. It was probably better not to have Sam involved in this, she told herself and willed herself to believe it. Things were only going to get complicated. She should never have brought up the accident. It was obviously a big deal to him. And what would happen if he told her? What would she do with that kind of personal information? That emotional entanglement? In the cold light of day, with her heart back on track, she could safely say she didn't want that kind of intimacy with him. It would only make things...messy.

She could get a life without a fake boyfriend. In fact—she looked down at her knees—nothing said getting a life like a healthy tan. Though she would probably just burn her knees. She'd spent much of her childhood with a burned nose and burned knees and nothing but white white skin in between.

A shadow fell across Anna and the small café table she was sitting at. She squinted up into the bright California sunshine.

"Good God, Anna, are those your feet?" Camilla asked.

"They are." Anna stretched out her legs and pointed her toes.

"I never thought I'd see the day," Camilla murmured and sat down beside Anna with her cup of tea. Camilla in city casual was just as lovely and poised as business Camilla. She was wearing a pair of khaki pants and blue shirt with yellow embroidery from Goddess's casual line.

Anna pushed up her sunglasses and took another bite of her cinnamon roll.

"Me neither, frankly, but I don't have any other shoes." Camilla looked up skeptically and Anna shrugged. "Tennis shoes and business shoes, that's it."

"Saddest thing I ever heard," Camilla said and took a sip of her steaming tea. "A woman should have some shoes."

"Well, now I have flip-flops." Anna looked at her feet again and grinned. Really, they were so comfortable.

"It was a wonderful day the other day with you and Sam," Camilla said in what had to be the most leading question ever uttered by her classy boss.

"Yes, it was. And no, we are not serious. That is all I am going to tell you about Sam." She took a bite of her cinnamon roll to keep all the things she wanted to say from spilling out of her mouth. "How are things at Arsenal?"

"Fine," Camilla said quickly. Anna turned toward Camilla fiddling with the handle to her tea cup. Camilla did not fiddle. She did not evade Anna's eyes unless something was wrong.

"What's wrong?" She all but barked. This is what happened when people were forced on sabbaticals. Things fell apart.

"Nothing we can't handle, Anna, really." Camilla even put a calming hand on Anna's arm. But Anna was not easily fooled, which was exactly what Camilla was trying to do.

"It's Aurora, isn't it?" Aurora Milan, the high-strung, sometimes troublesome president of Goddess Sportswear.

Anna knew that this would happen. Aurora was not very good at change and, considering the amount of hand-holding Anna had done over the years with Aurora, she had figured that this little change in personnel would send Aurora right back to her tarot cards and tea leaves.

"Anna," Camilla snapped and Anna rolled her eyes. "It's handled and you aren't supposed to be thinking about work. End of discussion."

"But, she's got to..."

"Anna?"

Anna muttered something under her breath and ignored Camilla's arch look. They sipped their drinks in silence for a few moments. Finally, fueled by frustration and espresso, Anna took the bull by the horns.

"Camilla," she started, firmly. As she had been waiting for Camilla to arrive, she had drawn up some boundaries she was not ready to cross in terms of spa day. A woman needed boundaries or before she knew it she would be covered in mud, while a giant man or woman tied her in knots and ripped all the hair off her body.

Anna's new boundaries would prevent all of that.

"At no time today do I want to be naked."

The couple at the table next to them looked up and laughed, but Camilla's eyebrows just raised over the edge of her teacup.

"No?" Camilla asked, as she put her cup back in its saucer. *Who the* hell *uses saucers anymore?* Anna wondered.

"That will certainly make most of the day difficult."

"Difficult or not, I will not be naked." Anna stuck to her guns. "A woman's got to have boundaries."

Camilla watched her for a moment, then drained the last of her tea. "Let's go, sweetheart, we're going to be late."

They stood and collected their bags. "Look at those," Camilla said, pointing to flowers growing in a planter attached to the fence right in front of them. "Those are the most perfect hydrangeas I've ever seen, don't you think?" Camilla asked and Anna looked at her through narrowed eyes. There was every chance this was a test, if she said yes, Camilla might turn around and say, "Those are roses, you dummy, you'll never work at Arsenal again." Though she might be exaggerating and the flowers didn't look like roses, she wouldn't put anything past Camilla. So, in the end, Anna told the truth.

"I didn't even notice them," she admitted.

"We've got a lot of work to do." Camilla put her arm around Anna's shoulder and they headed down the street to the spa.

THE SPA WAS GORGEOUS, walking into its lovely stone and wood interior with the fountain and small pond in the middle of the foyer, Anna felt like she needed to whisper. The sound of her flip-flops snapping against the stone floor with every step was very embarrassing in all of the tranquil silence. A woman sat at a desk just a few feet from the trickling fountain. Past the fountain and the receptionist desk, there was a large red door at the end of a long hallway.

Anna wondered how many times the receptionist had to go to the bathroom during the day listening to all that running water. Anna just walked in the door and she had to go.

"Hello, Ms. Lockhart," the receptionist greeted them in a voice just above a whisper.

"My daughter couldn't make it today, so I brought Anna." Camilla turned to Anna with a smile that Anna returned. She was kind of getting into the spirit of things here. She could deal with a little tranquility, a little pampering by the people behind that big red door. Within said boundaries, of course.

"Wonderful." The receptionist opened the gorgeous wooden armoire behind her and pulled out slippers placed on top of thick plush white robes.

"What...ah, what am I scheduled for here today?" Anna

asked and watched as Camilla and the receptionist shared a look.

"The works," they said in unison.

The big red door opened and Anna was introduced to Magda, a small, lean woman with skin the color of brazil nuts. Magda took Anna by the hand and led her through the mysterious inner workings of The Red Door Spa. She opened the door to what appeared to be a dark closet and gestured for Anna to enter.

"What's in there?" she asked the silent little woman point-blank.

"You remove clothing. Put on robe," Magda said with an indistinguishable accent.

"Yeah, then what?" Anna stared at Magda with narrowed eyes.

"Face, toes, fingers." Magda wiggled her fingers for emphasis. Anna nodded, thinking that sounded completely acceptable.

Twenty minutes after the beauty part of the day and the fully clothed part of the day finished, the torture part started. Wrapped in the plush white robe with her underwear firmly in place Anna met her "hair technician." Lai, a very small and polite but stubborn Korean girl, was having some serious trouble with Anna's boundary issues.

"Is so much easier..."

"I'm sorry, Lai. But I am leaving my underwear on."

"But..."

"I hear you, Lai, but it's no. Very much *no.*" Anna shook her head and crossed her arms over the lovely robe.

Thirty minutes later having lost the underwear battle, Anna was horrified and suffering in ways she had never imagined in this life. Having shown another woman parts of her body she herself had never seen, Anna was ready to call it quits on the whole spa day. But Magda, who had a grip like a steel claw, would not let Anna have her clothes back so she could leave.

"This will make you feel better," Magda assured Anna who was blinking back tears.

"I'm keeping my underwear on this time," Anna insisted. She had been violated enough.

Magda assured Anna that she could keep her underwear or at least, that's what Anna thought the woman said. But in the end, underwear meant nothing when one was forced to sit in a giant vat of warm mud.

They were in place, her cotton underwear, for the fat lot of good it did her.

Sitting up to her chin in mud, she wondered what would happen if there was a fire drill.

Finally, the torture was over and—bow-legged, sore in places she didn't even want to think about and carrying her mud-soaked underwear in a plastic bag—Anna walked out the big red doors, vowing to never go back.

Tranquil. Ha! Pampering. Bull! These people should be sued.

"Look at you, Anna," Camilla cooed from her spot by the fountain. "You look wonderful."

"Let's get out of here," Anna hissed under her breath, trying to keep her clothes from rubbing up against the new hairless parts of her body.

She had been wrapped and rubbed and soaked in mud and blasted by hot water and then cold water. She had laid on hot stones—which, in all honesty, wasn't that bad—but Lai and her evil hot wax had pretty much colored the whole experience.

"Your skin is just glowing." Camilla continued to chatter as they made their way past the fountain. "Really, you look years younger."

"It's because all my skin has been ripped away," Anna griped. "You're looking at my baby skin."

Everything was *tight*. Her skin, her pores, everything felt stretched and stripped and unbearably sensitive. And naked. Very, very naked.

The fact that she was walking around without underwear didn't help matters.

Camilla pushed open the door and sunshine hit them with all the intensity of a red-hot heat lamp. Anna slid her sunglasses on and wished she had a hat. Her poor skin was going to burn up. She hurried down the street as quickly as she could being bow-legged and flip-flopped.

"Anna?" Camilla put a hand on her arm and stopped her. People continued to walk past them on the busy sidewalk so Camilla took steps out of the way and Anna, without a choice, followed. "Anna? What's wrong?"

"I'll tell you what's wrong," Anna whispered furiously. "Hot wax is wrong. Hot wax is wrong in a million ways, Camilla."

Camilla laughed, not one of her cultured business laughs, but one of her family picnic laughs—loud and booming—and as people walked by, they turned to look at her as she leaned against the wall making merry at Anna's expense.

"I take it you didn't like..."

"Yeah, no. I didn't like."

"What about the rest of it? The baths and the hot stones?"

Anna took a deep breath. "Fine, I liked that fine, but I don't feel any need to do any of it again."

Camilla pushed away and made her way back into the stream of people on the sidewalk. "That's too bad, sweetheart, because you look like a new woman."

"There is no new woman, it's still me just chaffed. Can we get out of here?"

Anna grimaced and took up her bow-legged shuffle while Camilla followed. They were walking on the wrong side of the sidewalk, against all the foot traffic. But Anna barreled on, working her way up the sidewalk while everyone, it seemed, was trying to make their way down.

SAM SLOWED his run down to a jog and finally a walk. He hit the button on his watch that stopped the counter and smiled at the time. *Not bad, old man, not bad.*

He took the T-shirt he had stuffed down the back of his running shorts and used it to wipe the sweat off his chest and shoulders. It was hot today. Not a cloud in the bright blue sky. Heat shimmered up from the pavement of the parking lot. He tried not to look at Anna's condo, tried not to see if he could see any sign of her. But he looked and he didn't see her. He didn't know whether he should feel good or bad about that. He unlocked his own door, pushed it open and heard the phone ringing.

Having no idea where he left the damn thing, he followed the ringing until he found the phone on the windowsill in the bathroom.

"Hello?"

"Sam!"

Sam smiled and cringed at the same time. His sister, Angela, had that kind of effect on people. "Hey, Angie, what's up?"

"Sam." The tone of her voice had him putting down the toilet cover to have a seat. He knew he had it coming, but it never made being scolded any easier to deal with. "Do you realize how long it's been since you've called or stopped by?"

A month, almost exactly. "No," he said feigning innocence. "A few weeks?"

"Nice try. Watch it, Steven," she shouted to her son. Sam grinned wondering what the kid was getting into at the moment. When it came to trouble, his nephew was ingenious. He should introduce the kid to Anna's Meg. The kids would burn down San Francisco. "It's been a month, Sam. A month."

"I hadn't realized," he sighed and rested his shoulder against the sink. He looked in the bowl and snapped upright.

How long had it been since he had cleaned his john? It was gross. He reached into the small space under the sink cabinet and pulled out some cleaner and a sponge.

"Well, I'm letting you know that if you aren't at Sunday dinner, you might just be disowned. Steven." His sister didn't move the phone to yell at her son and Sam winced as her volume nearly ruptured his eardrum. Angela had always been a yeller. He sprayed the porcelain and scrubbed. "I am warning you."

"Who, me or Steven?" Sam asked.

"Both of you," she laughed, then paused. Sam closed his eyes waiting for it. The Drynan guilt. "Sammy, we miss you," she said and Sam's shoulder's fell as he gave in to the guilt.

"I'll be there Sunday."

"You used to come to every Sunday dinner," Angela started and Sam itched to get off the phone. "But since the accident you act like we're lepers or something."

"That's not true," he sighed.

"It's absolutely true, Sam. We're worried…"

"Well, don't be," he snapped, throwing the sponge in the sink. "I'll see you Sunday."

There was a pause and he knew that she knew that if she pushed, he wouldn't come. His entire family had all pushed right after the accident. Constant pushing and caring and worrying, all of them, so damned concerned and loving and smothering that he had just…disengaged. They didn't push too much anymore. But then he wasn't around much.

"Okay, Sammy," she said in a strong voice. "We'll see you Sunday."

They each hung up and Sam finished scouring the sink before he moved on to the rest of the bathroom, possessed by a need to do something, anything but think about his family and his accident and Anna. Mostly Anna.

Finally, he ran out of things to clean so he put away the

stuff and rubbed his face with his hands. Sweat was pouring off of him and he reached into the shower to turn it on.

He didn't want to talk to anyone. He didn't want to answer questions about how he was. How his recovery was progressing. He didn't want to see sympathy and pity in his little sister's eyes. In his mother's eyes. He was just glad his father had died before all of this happened. Seeing pity and sympathy in the old man's eyes would have ended him.

He stepped in the shower and hissed as the cold water hit his back. He quickly adjusted the temperature and as the warm water ran over him he sighed, ducking his head under the stream.

Hadn't he had enough? Wasn't it enough that he was never going to be able to do his job again? How much more did a man have to suffer?

And now Anna. It was outrageous what she expected from him. It wasn't fair what she wanted. He was a fake, on-call boyfriend. She couldn't expect anything more from him, such as swapping confessions. He squeezed shampoo into his hands and soaped up his hair. What did it even matter what she knew about him? Nothing. He wanted to get laid, not bare his soul. Nope. The price of admission into her bed was too high. Way too high.

He rinsed his hair and watched the soap slide down the drain and finally stopped pretending. He wasn't kidding anybody, pretending to be mad at her. Pretending that this was her fault.

"I was in an accident," he said out loud, hating the way the words echoed in the shower. "I broke my back and have some degenerative problems and I'll never be able to be a firefighter again."

He took a deep breath and let the water trickle into his mouth, filling it before he spat it out at the drain.

"I hate my life," he whispered and closed his eyes to the spray hitting his face.

He felt so bad about saying the things he had said to Anna. He had spent a sleepless night knowing that she was right and that he couldn't keep stonewalling her while trying to get her naked at the same time. It was mean and disrespectful. He got that.

He also knew that he had no right to judge her life as boring. At least she was going after something she wanted. At least she knew what she wanted.

He couldn't even say that much. He was mad and frustrated and had taken it out on her.

He was thirty-four. Thirty-four and he felt like his life had already been lived. It was over. The guys at the house and his family kept telling him that there were a lot of options for a man in his position. Sam snorted at the idea and accidentally got a nose full of water.

He put his hands up on the wall by the spigot so the water hit the back of his neck. He groaned and flexed his shoulders. Options? For a guy like him? Sam tried to think about it— something that a few months ago he couldn't even try. This idea of options was like poking at a bad bruise, if he got too close, it hurt so he shied away. He tried to imagine himself behind some desk and the idea was awful. He shook his head. There had to be something else. Something else mildly fulfilling, because his life was stretching out into an endless workout and struggle to fill his days.

If it weren't for this thing with Anna, he didn't know what he would do. If it weren't for Anna... He grinned and tilted his face up into the spray. He had expected a challenge. A distraction, but Anna was turning into something else. Something more.

He smiled as he soaped up his armpits.

He would apologize. He would apologize and tell her about the accident. He could do that. He wanted to do that. If that was what it took to spend time with her, then, of course, he could do it.

He pushed aside thoughts of the fire department and his life and focused on Anna. The heavy pressure he felt almost every minute of every day vanished and he hurried through the shower so he could chase her down and get her to laugh and, if he was lucky, get her to make out with him against some door.

ANNA WANTED NOTHING more than to just crawl into her bed and apologize to her poor skin. Maybe she would order in something fattening...fried chicken would make her skin feel much better. She turned the corner toward her house and saw Sam sitting on her front stoop.

It was ridiculous what her heart did. The crazy leap. The strange squeeze of her belly. He saw her coming and stood up slowly, like some kind of fantasy, like an advertisement for something impossibly sexy.

"Hey, Anna," he said when she got to the bottom step.

"Hi, Sam." She smiled back tentatively. They had not talked since the other night and she wasn't sure what was about to happen. There was every chance he was here to tell her some more about her dull and sterile life. And she really didn't think she could take any more of that. "How are you?" she asked.

"Tired, I didn't sleep very well last night."

"Me either," she admitted. "I feel awful about—"

"Two years ago there was a house fire up in California on the 'Loin,'" he said quickly interrupting her. "In the old rowhouses up there. Someone left a stove on...." He coughed and swallowed and Anna held her breath. "We had gotten everybody out. We thought we had everything under control, but some of those old houses have attics that are connected and the fire spread to a house next door." He stopped and rubbed his neck, his eyes wouldn't meet hers, but it didn't matter. She just couldn't believe he was doing this. "It just went up like...I don't know. I had never seen anything like that. Well, there was a family... A woman came out, screaming that her husband and daughter were still in there, so we went in..." He cleared his throat again. "I, ah...I went in. The man was passed out in the hallway from the smoke so I grabbed him and got him out and then I went back for the little girl. Her bedroom was upstairs beneath the corner of the roof that had caught first. It was..." His eyes met hers and she wanted to tell him that he didn't have to say any more, but he barreled on. "It was pretty bad. I found her, but getting out was tough. I heard the roof start to go and my instincts were wrong and in the smoke I went one way when I should have gone the other and...the roof came down on us."

She grabbed his hand and he gripped hers hard and she wanted to tell him to stop. She didn't know what to do with this confession. This trust and intimacy he was giving her, but she couldn't open her mouth to stop him. The words poured out of him and she could only listen and feel things crumble as she tried to handle his pain.

"They found us. The girl was okay, scared mostly. But I was in pretty bad shape." The corner of his mouth curled up in a half grin. "And that's what happened. That's..." He blew out a long breath and laughed, a rueful bark that was far more pain than pleasure.

"I wanted to tell you that and I wanted to tell you how sorry I am for the other night."

Anna ducked her head and felt the tears in her eyes.

"You're a hero," she whispered, rooted to the spot when she really just wanted to run away.

"No," he said firmly. "No, I am not. I was just good at my job. Like you." He pushed up her sunglasses and she blinked in the sunshine, the tears pooling in her eyes. "You're the—" he stopped and his eyebrows snapped together.

"What?" He shut his mouth and swallowed and Anna took the first step to stand in front of him. She grabbed his arm, thinking that he really didn't look too steady on his feet. "What's wrong?"

"What happened to you?" he breathed, his eyes darting over her face. "You look..." He stopped, swallowed again and she watched his eyes as they traveled over her face. Her newly sandblasted and mud-packed skin preened under his scrutiny. He smiled again, that half grin, and put his hands on her shoulders, his thumbs curving along her collarbones. "I know we're just fake dating and everything, I know that we don't really know each other, but I am going to say this..."

He paused and Anna drowned, absolutely drowned in his expression.

"You're the most..." He stopped and Anna blinked. He looked away and cleared his throat. *Come on. Come on you can do it.* "You look..." He stopped again. Anna leaned in closer. Maybe he just needed a little encouragement.

"Sam...?"

"You are so pretty." He finally blurted out. "Really—" he kept going "—very pretty."

Anna laughed. She couldn't help it. Were they in sixth grade? Pretty. She had been tortured for hours to get to "pretty." She knew she was no Marie, but come on. The man wanted to get into her pants, she had to be more than pretty. Didn't she?

"I mean...hey," he was saying and Anna kept laughing. "You're always pretty, but now... Come on, I'm serious, Anna."

"Okay, sorry. But, pretty?" She laughed again, he was no good with the compliments.

He cupped her cheeks in his hands and lifted her on her toes. Her laughter stopped as he kissed her. His tongue stroked her lips and she let him in and melted against him. Her hands went around his waist and pulled him closer as she sank deeper into his kiss. Deeper into what was happening between them.

"You are beautiful," he whispered against her lips and her eyelids fluttered closed. His mouth trailed across her skin to her ear. "You are gorgeous," he breathed and her nipples hardened in a painful rush. "You..." He kissed her forehead. "You amaze me."

She sank against him, pressing her face against his chest. Sam cupped her neck and held her snug to his body. Anna ridiculously fought back tears. Nobody ever, ever had said such things to her and, while she wanted to be above it, she wasn't. Inside, parts of her that had never been tended properly and grew wild and thorny with insecurity, turned toward this new light in her life.

Sam.

"Let's go see a movie," he said, kissed her head and grabbed her hand to lead her away but she stopped him, a question clawing its way out of her suspicious and distrustful nature.

"Wait a second." He turned back to look at her. "Did you tell me this just to get in bed with me?"

He shook his head. "I told you because I wanted to tell someone. I...ah...I wanted to tell you."

Danger! Danger, Anna Simmons.

Every instinct told her to say no. To say forget the whole thing, but in the end she couldn't. All day long she had been miserable thinking she wouldn't see him again. And now he was here, sexy and smiling and wanting to take her to a movie. How could she say no. Besides, she rationalized, what would a movie hurt?

"Just a second." She opened her apartment door. "Wait right there." She ran into her bedroom, yanked on a pair of cotton underwear. She dumped her bag of muddy underwear in the garbage and headed back out to the porch and Sam.

"Ready," she said and grinned at him.

He took her hand and she followed without a word. With clean underwear and her heart faltering with new feelings, she followed him.

10

ANNA STARED HARD at the phone. Ever since her brief conversation with Camilla about Aurora and what was going on at Arsenal, Anna had been getting more and more stressed about what was happening without her there. She could call Aurora, explain the situation and put the woman's mind to rest. Or she could just call Andrew Boyer and threaten his life if he screwed this up. That would be very satisfying.

She picked up the phone to call Aurora. And quickly hung up. If Camilla found out she had called, she would be in serious trouble. On the other hand, Anna had a vital stake in the future of Arsenal, a future that she believed banked almost entirely on Goddess Sportswear and the contract she had spent the past six months of her life sweating over.

With that little nudge of righteous indignation, she picked up the phone and called Aurora Milan's number.

"Goddess Sportswear," the receptionist answered coolly.

"Aurora Milan," Anna said trying to disguise her voice an octave lower, which she recognized as pretty stupid. But these were desperate times.

"She's in a meeting, can I take a message?"

Shit, Anna hadn't anticipated that. "Uh...no thanks," she stammered and hung up.

She flopped back onto her couch and stared up at her ceiling. She needed something to distract her from this mess. She looked at her watch. Sam was teaching little kids basketball at the Y and Marie was no doubt sanding floors or sewing curtains or something equally unpleasant—Anna wanted nothing to do with that. She looked around her spotless apartment. Since getting the cleaning woman she couldn't even distract herself with her own filth.

Anna chewed on the nail of her middle finger.

She had been prepared to play by Camilla's rules and stay out of things for six months. Anything to get her job back. Anything for Arsenal. But surely if Aurora was getting upset, Anna had obligations to get involved.

She called her assistant, Jen. But she wasn't there. Anna couldn't stop herself and so to prevent a complete breakdown, she called Camilla's assistant, Emily. It was a risk, but the woman knew everything that happened at Arsenal and she was easily bought. Like any good hustler, which Emily was in her heart of hearts, she kept her mouth zipped when there was something in it for her. Anna already owed the woman a month of meals at Marie's, what was another month?

"Camilla Lockhart's office."

"Emily?" Anna whispered.

"I'm sorry, I can't hear you."

"Emily," she said in a louder voice.

There was a pause, then Emily started whispering, "You could get into a lot of trouble calling here, Anna."

"Yeah, I know, but what's going on there? Where's Jen?"

"She gets a month paid vacation for having put up with you for so long."

Anna gasped, outraged. Then shocked. Then she grimaced. There *had* been a lot of late nights and a lot of irrational runs to get more peanut butter cups. The girl deserved some time off. "Okay. That makes sense," she told Emily. "But what's going on with Aurora at Goddess."

"I don't know," Emily answered. "But Andrew has spent the last three nights sleeping on the couch in your office...."

"He's in my office?" Anna squawked.

There was another pause. "You didn't know?"

"No, I didn't know! Is the world coming to an end around there? Andrew is in my office?"

"Well, it gets worse. Yesterday Camilla had me send Aurora flowers."

Anna stood up, her skin prickled in an awful rush of panic. "Flowers?"

"Yeah, they were..." Anna could hear Emily rifling through papers. Anna closed her eyes and prayed that Camilla had sent daisies. Aurora was a total whack job and would forgive most things for a bouquet of daisies.

"Roses," Emily said finally.

"Roses?" Anna gasped, horrified. Anything but roses. Lilies, sunflowers, anything...but roses. Oh, God.

"Yeah, red roses," Emily confirmed.

"This is a disaster," Anna breathed. "Daisies, you're supposed to send daisies." But nobody was there to tell Camilla that. Anna was gone, Jen was gone. Arsenal was shooting into the dark without them there.

"Why?"

"Because nobody knows that woman like I do," Anna said, her fist clenched at her side. "Because in all the years I have known her, I have sent her bouquets of daisies, because they are her freakin' happy flower." Anna was losing it. She could feel it. She put her thumbnail in her mouth just to calm herself down. She was too uninformed. Too out of the loop. That was going to have to change. "Look, Emily, you have to got to keep me posted."

"Well." Emily paused and Anna could hear the beat of her mercenary heart. "It'll cost you."

"What? What will it cost me?"

"Marie's recipe for the tiramisu she served at the Christmas party."

Anna winced. Marie guarded recipes like the holy grail. Anna worked on the cuticle of her pinky finger. "You sure you wouldn't rather..."

"Recipe or you're in the dark."

"Fine," Anna breathed. "I'll get it for you." How, she had no idea. As far she knew Marie kept her recipes in a safe deposit box or under her mattress or in her bra or something.

Anna hung up the phone, feeling nothing but dread. Things were worse than she could have ever dreamed.

What to do, what to do? She drummed her fingers against the pale blue fabric of her couch and chewed on the nails of her freehand. But as things lined up in her brain, obstacles that needed to be dealt with, tasks and objectives, she felt a certain gathering of her will. Even worrying about work felt a whole lot better than doing nothing all damn day.

She checked her watch. She had just enough time before she was supposed to meet Marie for something called Pilates. She dug under her butt for the remote control that was buried in the cushions. The amnesia victim, Cheyenne was supposed to remember her past today on the daytime soap Anna was *not* addicted to. She just wanted to see Hunter's face when he realized Cheyenne was his long-lost, evil-twin brother's wife.

"THEY'RE JOKING with this, right?" Sam asked. He took a step closer to the green canvas on the wall and looked back at Anna. "It's a joke right?"

Anna shrugged, laughing. Sam was not enjoying the San Francisco Museum of Modern Art. He came back to stand next to her, bending close to her ear. "It's just green paint on canvas."

She and Sam were here to run into Camilla and Michael who were members of the museum and came religiously every other Saturday. Bumping into Camilla and Michael at the museum with Sam's hand in hers would be huge. Huge.

Maybe she would get even a few more minutes to grill Camilla about what was happening at Arsenal. Anna had spent some time at the Starbucks across the street from Arsenal hoping to ambush Andrew there, and get the scoop from him, but the man never seemed to leave the building.

Sam continued to look at the huge canvas, unable to hide his baffled dislike. "I could do this shit."

Anna tugged on his hand. "I don't think you are allowed to swear in art museums," she whispered.

"I don't think this is art," he whispered back.

"Okay, then Mr. Expert, what do you consider art?" she challenged him, enjoying herself immensely.

She didn't particularly like what they had seen, either. The building was easily the most interesting thing about the museum so far. Large, light and airy with its distinctive cylindrical atrium in the middle, it was awe-inspiring just walking in. She certainly could appreciate that the paintings she was looking at were art to someone, just not her.

And apparently not to Sam. Green canvases and sculptures of legs with human hair sticking out of the wall did not impress Sam. She had thought he liked the Jackson Pollacks because he was so silent looking at them, but then he'd turned to her and said, "It's just squiggles."

She had to nod because, frankly, that was all she saw, too. She wondered what Camilla saw in this stuff. Anna wondered what the guy across the room who had been staring at the canvas painted red for twenty minutes saw in this stuff.

"Okay," Sam said, taking up her challenge. He grabbed her hand and marched over to a map of the museum. He grinned, his green eyes alive with humor and a certain amount of boyish mischief that thrilled her. He practically dragged her up the stairs past a painting of squares, another one of squiggles and a big pile of rope coiled up on the floor and finally, into a section they had not visited. Photography.

After the rooms of obscure paintings and strange "sculptures" it was a relief. Literal and real, the photos in their stark black-and-white beauty engaged her brain and she sighed.

"Wow," she breathed.

"Yeah, wow," he breathed back. They slowly made their way past the captured moments of reality.

Anna stood in front of a picture of a woman's twisting torso. It was gorgeous, the play of light over skin and breasts, the shadows of feminine muscles. The photo next to it was of a woman's closed eye and even that seemed somehow ultra feminine.

"Dirty pictures," Sam said with a smile.

"I like these," she whispered.

"Me, too," he whispered back. He brushed the hair off her neck and she braced herself for the touch of his lips against her skin, but she was still surprised. Surprised by the reaction in her body to just that small touch. He chuckled in her ear and kissed her neck again.

"Someone should take a photo of this," he said, tracing the length of her neck. "I swear you've got the most beautiful neck I've ever seen."

"Sam," she whispered, prepared to tell him that he didn't need to say those things. After he had told her about the accident and they went to a movie she discovered the boundaries between them were vanishing. The rules regarding public displays of affection that she had established in her mission statement were forgotten in the warmth of his touch and the rumble of his laugh.

"Well, look at this," a man said in a voice a little over a whisper. Anna and Sam both turned and there was Michael. He grinned and pushed his stylish glasses up his nose. "Last person I ever expected to see here," he chuckled as he leaned in to kiss Anna's cheek, then he shook Sam's hand.

"You know something, half the stuff out there is just plain dumb in my mind, but this..." Michael said, gesturing toward the photos, "Well, this is something isn't it?"

"Yep," Sam said. He put an arm around Anna and kissed the side of her head. "This is art to me."

Anna smiled up at Sam and for a moment the world fell

away. Arsenal. Aurora. Camilla. All of it vanished and she was so happy to know him. She felt...good. Not about the work she did or about what she had accomplished, he made her feel good about her neck! Her neck, of all things. He made her feel funny and appreciated more than her to-do list.

She should have stopped him from telling her about the accident. Ever since that moment things had been different between them. Closer. Intimate.

She just wanted to know him better. She wanted to know what he was scared of and what he wanted to be when he was a kid. Even more, she suddenly wanted to tell him about her family. About moving and feeling lost. She wanted to tell him about Jim and the Q-Tips. About being scared of heights and wishing that she could play the piano.

And that was more terrifying than the prospect of losing her job. She swallowed hard against the lump of panic that had instantly appeared in her throat.

She laughed awkwardly and pushed herself away from Sam. "Is Camilla with you?" she asked Michael.

"Yeah, she's looking at something called 'mixed media.'" He shook his head at the words.

"I'll..." She looked back at Sam and he didn't seem to be noticing her, his eyes on the photos. "I'll go find her and say hi," she said. Sam turned toward her, nodded and winked before looking back at the art. That conspiratorial wink, the "we're in this together and isn't it working out great" wink, sent her reeling.

"Okay, I'll meet up with you in a half hour." He tilted his head as he looked at the photo of the twisting woman. "I think I see nipple."

"Really?" Michael asked adopting Sam's tilted head pose.

Adolescent monkeys, Anna thought in an effort to pull herself away from the strange allure Sam had over her. She couldn't lose focus, she couldn't be distracted by Sam. But as she turned around for just one last look at him—tall and strong and handsome—Anna realized that it was already too late. The question was, what was she going to do now?

She walked out of the photo exhibit and found a map. After a few deep breaths, she figured out where she was and how to get to where she wanted to be.

"HELLO, ANNA?" Sam snapped his fingers in front of Anna's face and she shook her head, dragging her eyes away from the middle distance she had been staring into. Sam's leg was pressed against hers in their little booth and she had been concentrating on the feel of his skin against hers. Well, initially she had been concentrating on moving her leg away from his, but then she had gotten all caught up in it.

"You with me?" he asked, leaning into her face.

"Yeah, sorry, just thinking." She smiled and looked down at the table filled with food. It was a few hours after their "run-in" with Camilla and Michael. Sam had demanded a burrito after the art museum. He even made her pay, insisting that she owed him.

Anna scrubbed at a spot of dried salsa on the table from the people that had been there before them. They were at his favorite place, Mi Fiesta. An old man named Hector and his wife owned the variety store-gas station-restaurant and Sam ruled there was no better burrito in all of Northern California than Mi Fiesta.

Anna seriously doubted that. Food should not be bought out of a gas station. It should be a rule. But he disagreed and now they were sitting in a dirty booth on the back porch of the gas station eating off wax paper.

Anna eyed her burrito and started to open up the flour tortilla. She just couldn't blindly bite into the dumb thing, she had to know what was in there. She had ordered chicken, but that didn't necessarily mean chicken was in it.

"You don't want to do that," Sam told her. He put his hand on hers to stop her.

"I just want to see what's in it."

He shook his head. "Better to not know. Trust me, it's delicious." He smiled at her, his lips shiny and wet from the beer he was drinking. He took another big bite from his own burrito and things low in Anna's belly clenched tight. He was so loose and casual. So easy and comfortable, it made her very aware of how tightly coiled she was.

She watched him for a minute more, the muscles in his shirt bunching as he lifted his burrito and then his beer to his mouth. His jaw, his throat both moved. He smiled at her, part challenge and part serious enjoyment and Anna wanted some of what came so easily to Sam.

She took a deep breath, lifted her burrito and took a bite.

Flavors, hot and sort of sweet and exploded in her mouth. "Oh, my God," she muttered through a full mouth, looking down at the mysterious fillings of her burrito.

"I know. It's awesome, isn't it?"

"Yeah, it is," she agreed and took another bite.

More people filed onto the patio. A dog came up and sniffed at Anna's toes. The breeze kicked up around them, swirling leaves and stirring up the smells of the food. Sam leaned forward and opened up a plastic container on their table. Inside were a bunch of carrots and cauliflower and green peppers floating in some clear liquid that smelled sharp and hot. Sam used the tongs to pull out some of the vegetables and put them on his piece of wax paper. He lifted one of the carrots with his fingers and held it out to her.

"Try it," he told her.

She reached up to take it from him and he pulled his hand back and jerked his chin up. Anna's breath came up short. He wanted to feed her. *Feed her*? And, oh God, she wanted him to do it.

She leaned forward, opened her mouth and he slowly put

the tip of the carrot slice in her mouth. She didn't look at his face, couldn't, as she used her teeth to pull the whole thing into her mouth. He resisted and she pulled a little more. It was all the most erotic thing ever.

Until her entire mouth felt like a gasoline fire.

"Haaaaaa," she breathed through her open mouth. She grabbed her beer and drained it. "You didn't say it was going to be hot!" She grabbed his beer and took little sips until the fire cooled enough that she could feel her lips. Sam laughed and began shoveling some of the pickled hot vegetables into his own mouth.

The sexy mood was ruined. *Did he mean that?* That sexy moment between them? Or did he mean to ruin that sexy mood? *Was all of this on purpose?* She wondered, watching him act as if nothing out of the ordinary had happened. Maybe it hadn't. Maybe she was reading into things.

Are you overanalyzing a man eating a burrito? Yes. Yes, you are. She waited for her mouth to cool down before eating anything more. Her lips and tongue were tingling with the heat of the spicy carrot.

"So what did Michael say after I left?" Anna asked, getting her mind away from Sam and erotic sexy things and back on the real issue at hand. She took another bite of her burrito.

"He said—" Sam lifted his eyebrows "—that he, could see nipple, too."

Anna shook her head at him. "Come on, really."

"What do you think he said, Anna?" Sam asked. "He grilled me about us." He took his beer back and waggled it between the two of them.

"So?" Anna asked.

"So, what? I told him we were casually dating."

"Oh." She took a breath before picking up her burrito again.

"How did it go with Camilla?" he asked.

"It went pretty well. Until I brought up Arsenal."

"That's not a surprise." He looked at her out of the corner of his eye as he took a bite, then leaned back to chew and swallow. He stretched his long legs out in front of him and again Anna was pressed against him all along the side of her leg. "Why'd you bring it up?"

"Because," she sort of snapped, feeling tense from Sam and Camilla and what was happening at Arsenal without her. "I'm concerned. Because it's what I do."

"Well, you're supposed to be fired, so I'd stop asking for trouble," he told her. It made a lot of sense. She *should* do that. She just didn't think she could.

He reached across the table to cup her cheek and his thumb rubbed the suddenly unbearably sensitive skin at the corner of her lips.

"Salsa," he murmured, then he licked the salsa from his thumb. Anna wondered for a second how she could accidentally spill salsa all over her body.

ANNA AND SAM wandered up the sidewalk toward their condos and she steeled herself for the advance he was going to make. She felt so weak with wanting him.

What is wrong with doing this? she asked herself. *Sleep with him, you don't have to be a saint or a martyr. Do what you want, instead of what you think.*

The fact was, life was going to go back to normal. After the sabbatical, things would go right back to what they were before. She'd had no time for a relationship before and she wasn't going to again. The relationship part of this situation was really over before it even started. Which, frankly, only left the naked parts.

Hell, yes! Her body screamed and heated up to a boiling point.

Yeah, she would sleep with him. He just needed to say the word. What would it hurt? Nothing.

"Anna?" Sam asked, from behind her as they strolled up the concrete.

Naked, naked, naked, her body chanted.

"Yes," she whispered in the night air that was so lush and warm and filled with opportunity.

He touched her elbow under the sleeve of the white button-up shirt she was wearing. She turned around to face him. The lights of the small parking lot in front of their condos lent a warmth to the night. A mellow glow that fell across Sam's face and turned his skin golden.

The lilac bushes that grew around Sam's doorstep perfumed the air and Anna knew that the night was truly ripe for seduction.

Or screwing him up against the door. Don't forget that option! Anna felt herself blush with all the things she wanted from this man. All the things she wanted him to do to her.

"I...ah," he chuckled uncomfortably and looked down at his feet for a moment. "I have a favor to ask you."

"Sure," she said softly wondering what he wanted and hoping that it was dirty. After five years she was so very, very ready for dirty.

"This Sunday would you mind going to a family dinner with me?"

"Family dinner?" she asked as her dirty little thoughts plummeted.

"Yeah, I thought this fake dating thing could go both ways." He sighed and smiled a tight little smile and Anna realized he was uncomfortable. That surprised her. Sam was not what she would consider an uncomfortable guy.

Say no, her brain told her. *Keep it simple stupid. Sex and getting your life back, that's it.* This thing was getting away from her. Before Sam's little burrito foreplay, the goals had been just getting her job back. If she added the sex and the family, the floodgate would open and there was no telling what other sort of intimacy might creep in. She should really say no.

"Just a few hours," he said. "It would really help me out."

"Of course," she said and he smiled, obviously relieved.

"Great, that's great, Anna. I'll try to keep them under control."

She laughed, not sure what he meant. "No problem."

"So, tomorrow then?" he asked. Anna was bewildered by this strange change in him. He was at least a foot away and he gave no, absolutely no, indication of getting any closer.

"Tomorrow," she agreed and watched while Sam turned and walked away without so much as an attempted good-night groping. What was this new game Sam was playing? Had she missed her shot? Was it over? While her mind was busy trying to figure out what was going on with the man, her body had taken a few steps toward his porch where he stood unlocking his door.

"Everything okay?" he asked, his brow furrowed in concern.

Nooooooo! her body howled. *No, it's not. I'm dying here.*

"Anna?"

Here it was—her chance. But in the end, she was a total failure.

"No, nothing. Good night, Sam." She finally turned and walked away listening to her body berate her for a coward.

SAM UNLOCKED his door and looked sideways as Anna snapped herself out of her reverie and walked toward her own home.

Gotcha, he thought and smiled wickedly.

11

IT WAS ONE of the rare times when Anna let Sam drive. He made the most of it by making her a little bit nervous.

"Were you the guy who drove the fire truck?" she asked, clutching the door handle of his sporty two-seater as he braked at the last second behind a moving van.

"Naw," he said casually, knowing she was struggling not to tell him to slow down. "They wouldn't let me."

He thought he heard her say, "I can see why" under her breath and so he took a tight corner and revved his car up to fourth gear.

"Sam..." she squeaked as they merged with traffic, heading north of the city.

"My folks live out of town, it takes a few minutes to get there," he told her. Her hair was blowing out of her ponytail in the wind that was coming through her open window. Some of the strands were so long he could feel them on his face in the close quarters of the car. They felt like feathers against his skin and he forced himself not to think about how all that hair would feel against the rest of his skin.

"So, Anna." He rolled up her window with the buttons on the console between them and turned on the fan so they could talk. "I think things are soon going to be lopsided between us." He smiled at her and knew she wasn't following him.

"After today, you are going to know quite a bit more about me than I do about you. My mom is probably going to show you some naked baby pictures of me."

"Oh, I hope so," she said, joking with an ease that he hadn't seen from her in their past few weeks together.

He took Highway 35 because he loved driving on the parts of it that hugged the water. As they eased out onto the road with sheer rock cliffs on one side and the bay on the other, he felt like he could breathe easier. Anna looked as though she felt the same, she grabbed some of the hair that had blown around and tucked it behind her ears in what was the most girlish gesture he had ever seen her make.

He suddenly wanted to take a trip with her. A road trip. Just the two of them, maybe go down to Santa Barbara for a weekend. They could go camping. He tried to imagine Anna camping and the idea so enchanted him that he chuckled.

"What would you like to know?" She turned a bit in her seat to better see him and he mentally rubbed his hands together with anticipation. He loved what her red T-shirt with the three little buttons at the collar did to her eyes and her hair.

She was Technicolor Anna and it made him want to pull over and kiss her.

"Where are your parents?" he asked. He glanced at her quickly and shifted up to fifth gear.

"I never knew my father and my mother is in Arizona."

Nice one. Go right for the sensitive subjects, he chastised himself.

"Do you ever see her?" he asked, thinking that his casual questions had opened up a can of worms.

"Not really." He looked at her again to see if this conversation was somehow uncomfortable for her. "I sort of declared my independence from her when I was eighteen and I don't think she ever forgave me."

"Declaration of Independence?" he asked. "That sounds serious."

Anna shrugged and wiped some hair from her lips as she stared out the window. "She wasn't a very good mom. She tried, but..." After a moment Anna continued, telling him how her mother had kept them moving every few years.

"That must have been pretty tough," he said and the comment sounded lame to him. He had no idea what to say. He had grown up in the house his father had grown up in. He had roots going deep into the soil of this area. He sped up and passed a VW van that was backfiring in the lane ahead of him.

"Well," Anna laughed. "I wasn't the most outgoing kid and it made it pretty impossible to make friends."

He could see her as a ten-year-old at her third new school in as many years. Uncomfortable and shy and only getting more so as time went by.

"Hey." She put a hand on his arm. "It's not that big of a deal. Lots of people move away from home. It's just usually the kids who do it and not the parents." She smiled warmly at him and he nodded his head. She told him how Marie had come to live with her and she had gotten the job at Arsenal and things had just gotten better from there.

"Wait a second," he said looking at her in amazement. "You're telling me you put yourself through college and worked your way up to president of Arsenal Advertising from being a secretary?"

"Not even a secretary," Anna said. "Receptionist. I just answered phones and cleaned up the boardroom."

"Anna..." He looked at her slack-jawed and, unaware of what to say, he put his hand on her head. Her hair was silky, her skull warm and small in his hand and he wobbled her head on her neck and she laughed a little. "You are something else, you know that?"

Anna looked away from him, a shy smile that went through him like lightning on her lips. "Thanks, Sam."

The silence had stretched between them. "Tell me about your family," she said. "Why do you need a fake date to Sunday dinner?"

"Because they are insane. They live for my love life, they just can't get enough of it," he said, enjoying the sound of her laughter, but pretending not to. "I'm not joking." Anna continued to laugh.

"When I show up without a date, they don't feed me. Anna, stop laughing, I'm serious." He wasn't, of course. Well, sort of. In the past few years his family did seem to go a little nuts asking whether there was someone special in his life. His sister, especially, was like a dog with a bone when it came to his love life.

"So, how many fake dates have you brought up here just so you can eat?" Anna asked, still laughing. But Sam suddenly sobered. He didn't know how to say this. He knew that the key to Anna was keeping things easy, light. He had to pretend that he wasn't falling for her and telling the truth here might ruin things.

But in the end he just couldn't lie.

"I haven't brought a girl home to meet my family in four years, Anna," he said and busied himself shifting down and taking the off-ramp toward his parents' house. He didn't look at her, but he could feel the surprise rolling off of her in waves.

Well, good, he thought a little bitterly. See how she felt dealing with this stuff.

ANNA QUICKLY counted the number of people in the kitchen. Six adults, four kids. Same as last count. Anna herself wasn't making any noise—she had barely said a word since walking into the modest bungalow in Atherton. Sam's brother-in-law, George, was also silent and even looked as though he might be sleeping. His balding head bobbed a bit and finally sank down to his chest. Anna couldn't believe it. How did someone sleep in the midst of all this noise?

Sam was answering the questions from the six different conversations he was engaged in.

"Johnny Manganello has no idea what he is talking about," he said to his mother who had claimed that this Johnny guy had a position for him at the firehouse.

"Well, would you look at that," he exclaimed for his smallest niece, a little dark-haired girl covered in grape Kool-Aid and holding up a Barbie for Uncle Sam to see. "Angela, could you please grab me a tissue or something?" He held out a hand and his oldest sister, Angela, a woman who seemed to be perpetually yelling, put a wash cloth in his hand. He grabbed one of his nephews around the waist as he raced past him.

"Steven, dude, you got to take care of this...." He swiped the wash cloth under Steven's runny nose and let the kid go.

Anna was completely exhausted and she had been here only twenty minutes.

"Do you like the wine?" Cindy, Sam's mother—a lovely diminutive blonde with more tasteful gold jewelry than was actually tasteful—asked politely. She gestured at Anna's wineglass when Anna only looked at her, shell-shocked by all the noise.

"I love it," Anna answered and quickly drank about half the glass down in one bracing gulp. Cindy sat down on the bench Anna had been planted on since arriving. This kitchen with its long table and modest appliances seemed to be the heart of this home and no one looked like they were going to leave despite, obviously, being crowded.

Angela and Sam's other sister, Jackie, were leaning against the counter yelling over the sounds of their children racing around the place, tripping over each other and the adults and a dog that, unbelievably, was lying down in the center of the yellow linoleum floor.

"So?" Cindy smiled, graciously, but Anna wasn't fooled. This was a mama shark coming after her for information. Anna sipped more of her wine. She wished Sam had prepped her for this. Had told her what she should say to these people who obviously were so concerned for their son and brother and so hopeful that she might be real. Which made sense if Sam hadn't brought home a woman to meet his family in years. Anna's heart leapt in reaction to that reality. Again, these things he was telling her, this intimacy he was piling on her head was uncomfortable. She felt as though she was wearing a tight collar or a sweater that was too hot.

"We are so glad you are here," Cindy said and even reached over and squeezed Anna's hand. "It's so good to see our boy..." Cindy looked back at Sam who was waking up George with a not-so-gentle shake and laugh. George laughed good-naturedly and the two men fell into conversation. Sam took a drink from his plastic tumbler of iced tea and Anna watched the bob of his throat.

"Well." Cindy turned back to Anna with bright eyes. "It's just good to have him here."

Anna squeezed Cindy's hand and smiled back. Sam could pick up the pieces later, she wasn't going to make this little woman cry. "I know what you mean," she said and started answering all of Cindy's questions with as much truth as she could bear to tell her, while avoiding the whole "I've been fired" story. Anna imagined that would not go over with her fake boyfriend's mother.

"We've only been..." Anna coughed. "Dating a few weeks."

"Really?" Cindy looked surprised. "Weeks?"

"Well," Anna pretended to think, wondering what the right answer here was. "You know, I guess it's been about two months, time just flies with Sam."

Cindy broke into a wide smile so Anna guessed she got that one right.

"Is he eating enough?" Cindy asked, watching her son across the room.

"All the man does is eat," Anna answered with complete confidence.

After a few moments of idle questions about Anna's life, Cindy dropped her voice and looked at Sam to make sure he wasn't listening to their conversation. Sam was involved in some kind of argument with his sisters.

"Has he told you about the accident?" Cindy asked, quickly.

"He has," Anna answered and was completely unprepared for the radiant smile Cindy gave her. Tears filled the older woman's eyes and she struggled a moment for composure.

"I am so glad," Cindy breathed and hugged Anna hard in her tiny little arms. Anna caught Sam's eye over his mother's shoulder and she could only shake her head at his baffled look. "I'm so glad," Cindy kept whispering and Anna thought the woman was crying softly into her hair.

IT WAS ALL déjà vu. Parking the car. The sweet smell in the air. The lights in the parking lot casting long dark shadows across Sam's face. They had done this before. This lush anticipation, the thrill in the pit of her stomach had all become familiar. Achingly so.

"Well." Sam ran his hand through his hair. "Thanks for going with me."

Anna had spent most of the drive home watching the sun sink behind the horizon and gathering the courage to make the move that Sam, since their last heated groping on the steps, seemed reluctant to make.

"I hope they weren't too much, you know…" he trailed off and shrugged.

"They were great," Anna assured him. The cocoon was back around them—darkness and intimacy and the soft smell of summer on the air, of grass that had been warmed by the sun. There was a whirring sound of insects and the occasional bird. Anna concentrated on all of it, wondering if Sam was going to do something to end the suspense or if she was going to have to take matters into her own hands. And if she were to take matters into her own hands, how exactly would that happen?

She smiled, thinking about inviting Sam in for a little PowerPoint presentation.

Hey, remember when we almost had sex against my door? Let's do that again.

Anna wished for the courage-inducing, fruity-pleasure of a Cosmopolitan.

Or ten.

She was going to make love to Sam. She was going to end the five-year long abstinence that was beginning to eat away at her. She was going to do it, she just needed to figure out how.

"Well, if you like loud nosy families, I guess they are great."

Nerves made her laugh a little louder than she had anticipated. A small animal in the bushes around her porch got startled and ran off into the night.

Nice, Anna. Scare away the wildlife. Very sexy.

"They love you," she told him, her voice a little quieter. She took a small step toward him so that they really were within arm's reach of each other. She waited, anticipating his hand skimming her waist or grabbing her hip. When they were at the museum with Camilla and Michael he had put his hand in her pocket and left it there.

Come on, do that. Do that.

Sam put his hands in his own pockets and looked up at the sky.

"Yeah, I suppose. Sometimes it's a bit much, you know?"

Beginning to feel a little desperate, she reached out to touch his shoulder, part comfort, part invitation. Because, frankly, she was a total idiot, the touch turned into a slug in the arm and he looked at her askance.

"Sorry," she mumbled. *Where was an earthquake when you needed one?*

"Anna?" he asked. She laughed, a nervous sort of Beavis and Butthead laugh, then forced herself to shut her mouth and be quiet. She wedged the toe of her shoe into the cracks of the sidewalk they were standing on and felt, again, as though she was a fifteen-year-old.

She had slept with two men in her life. One man had been ten years ago for about a year. The other had been five years ago in a barely remembered one-night stand. She worked. She slept. She ate peanut butter cups. She couldn't remember ever reading *Cosmo* magazine—she looked at the ads—or books about how to seduce a man. She was in the dark here and Sam, who usually took care of these sorts of things, was no help.

"Are you okay?" he asked.

"Do you want to come inside?" she asked feeling a sick sort of anguished hope.

His smile was slow and potent. He wasn't even touching her—his hands were still in his pockets—but that smile stirred up a lot of warm embers in her body. Embers that glowed and began to burn.

He took the step this time. His hands didn't touch her, but with her quick breath her chest touched his and that, was enough to kill her. She did it again, her eyes locked on his mouth and that smile.

"Are you inviting me, Anna?" he whispered and she felt all the hair on her neck lift in acute awareness of him.

"Of course," she whispered lightly. Or at least trying to be light. Trying not to betray the fact that her nipples were aching and she could feel the sudden almost painful emptiness between her legs.

"Anna," he chuckled and Anna struggled to keep her eyes

open. His hands cupped her face, speared lightly into the sides of her hair and she couldn't help it, she gasped at the contact. He forced her to look at him and she did, sort of blindly. Seeing him, but not really. All of her faculties were centered on keeping her knees from buckling. "Anna, are you *inviting* me?"

Oh. She remembered his part of the bargain from weeks ago. He wouldn't do anything she didn't invite him to do.

She laughed, helplessly. "Yes, Sam, I am *inviting* you."

"All right." He kissed the tip of her nose, the side of her face and then stepped back. "Let's go inside." She stood there, staring at him and the more she stared, the hotter his green eyes got. Those eyes of his were burning her, seeing through her clothes, seeing through her skin. "Anna," he breathed after a moment. "I am barely holding on here, get us inside that house."

House, yes. She turned, fumbled for her keys. Dropped them once, bent over to grab them and heard Sam groan behind her.

"You're trying to kill me."

She wished she could say yes. But any killing of him on her part was purely accidental. Nerves were chasing desire around her body and the combination was making her clumsy and thick and foolish.

She ran up the steps, got the door open. Sam was right behind her. She could feel him through her midgrade panic. He shut the door behind them. She flicked on the light as she walked into the living room. He flicked it off.

She got into the kitchen. Bright moonlight spilled through the window across the floor and part of the counter. "Do you want a drink? I've got—"

Sam spun her, roughly. Lifted her, set her on the counter and pressed himself between her legs. Hard. Hot. *Oh, wow.*

His mouth was there, swallowing her words, stealing her breath. He pulled back and the light from the window fell

across his face, across his eyes. Anna gasped at what she saw
there. The hunger, stark and naked, was shocking. Exciting
almost beyond bearing.

"Sam," she sighed and pulled him to her. She arched her
back, pressing her hips and her chest against him. She
wanted to open up his skin and crawl inside of him. She
moaned into his open mouth, melting, falling, dying for
every touch of him.

He groaned and his hands, rough and clumsy, started
pulling her clothes off. She lifted her arms and he dragged
her T-shirt over her head while she went to work on his
clothes. Unbuttoning his shirt, pulling it off his shoulders,
she was desperate for his beautiful skin so smooth and white
in the moonlight.

"Sam, you are so perfect," she breathed into his neck. She
pressed kisses to his collarbone, the muscle of his shoulder.
Her hands skimmed all that warm flesh, tracing the hard
contours of his back. She paused for a moment when she felt
his scar, the hard ridge that was so long and so wide.

His head bent for a moment, his fingers stilled on the clasp
of her bra. She leaned back to look into his eyes, wondering
where he was. Where he had gone as she touched him.

"Sam?" she whispered, more a breath really. Their eyes
locked in the shadowed kitchen. Both half-naked. Her hands
on his scar, his hands on her almost untouched skin.

The panic hit Anna like a fist. This was too much. Too
powerful. She couldn't handle this. She pulled back a tiny
bit, her eyes darting away from his. He growled low in his
throat and his hands curled around her hips pulling her
against him. He wrapped her legs around his waist, his erection fitted perfectly, magically against her.

His eyes on hers, forcing her not to retreat, to bear what he
was doing to her, he lifted his hips a little, pressed in harder
and Anna fell back against the cupboards. A cry garbled in
her throat. Any thought of too much was gone, burned up

and blown away like ash in her sudden and crushing need for *more*.

His fingers brushed her between their bodies. The hot, wet, seam of her body. The lush and desperate part of her that was now in control. Her mind vanished. It was all about what he could do to make the ache go away.

He jerked at the buttons to her pants, yanked at her zipper and suddenly his hand was there.

"Yes," she moaned. "Yes." She lifted her hips and her clothes were gone, the counter cold on the back of her thighs, hard against her hips. His fingers searched her in the moonlight. Traced her, learning her like a map. Her body clenched as his thumb found her clitoris and his fingers slid into her with breathless and perfect accuracy.

She reached behind her, her fingers gripping the handles to the cupboards and she offered herself up to him, pushed herself hard into his fingers. *Not enough, not enough. Make it stop,* she thought.*Make it stop.* It had been so long. So unbearably, painfully long and she could not take it another minute.

"Anna," he breathed and leaned down and with his fingers buried in her, he put his mouth to her breast and sucked her into his mouth. Hard. His teeth. His tongue. His fingers moved faster and Anna, breathless and naked in the moonlight, fell apart.

HE CARRIED HER boneless and limp in his arms. Her head on his shoulder, her legs around his waist.

He kicked open the door to her office, probably expecting her bedroom and instead finding her computer. He growled. She fluttered with her hand to the closed door across the hall. He kicked open that door and it smashed against the wall. Anna smiled against his skin. She felt drunk. Happy.

He threw her lightly on the bed and the headboard rattled against the wall. The old bedstead had a shelf along the top of the headboard where, nightly, she put a glass of water.

Last night's glass was still there and the moonlight reflected off the water and sent little prisms across the ceiling and walls.

I should move that, she thought. She leaned up to do just that and was distracted by Sam furiously undoing his pants. A button popped off and rolled onto the floor.

"Anna," he said, his eyes hard. Muscles clenched in his jaw, his throat and all down his body. "You're..." He was panting. Barely holding on. Anna could only watch him in wonder. "You're making me crazy."

Anna didn't think it possible after the earth-shaking, mind-blowing orgasm she had had in the kitchen, but her body woke up a bit. *Hmm?* It purred to life.

He pulled down his underwear and Anna's eyes opened wide.

Sam was built nothing, *nothing*, like Jim. He pulled a foil packet from his pants pocket, ripped it open with his teeth and rolled the condom onto his erection.

"Ahhh," she started to say. She thought maybe now would be a good time to bring up the fact that it had been a few years. Almost ten unbroken years of celibacy. One year of sex—during which Jim had never almost screwed her against a door or on her kitchen counters and Jim had *never* looked as...dangerous as Sam looked at this moment—preceded by eighteen years of celibacy. She was about to suggest that perhaps a few moments of recovery or maybe preparation might be in order before they proceeded.

Sam grabbed her ankles and she fell back on the bed as he pulled her toward him. He put his knee on the bed between her spread legs. His fingers brushed against her again.

"You're so wet, Anna," he breathed.

Yeah, wet and nervous, she wanted to say. But he was inside of her, huge and smooth and there was no more talking.

She watched the prisms from the water glass jerk and shimmy on the ceiling. The glass was banging lightly against the wall with every one of Sam's deep thrusts. It didn't hurt, not at all. It felt good, but not in any sort of way that was going to grow into anything else. His face was buried in the mattress beside her, his hands in her hair. His breath hard in her ear. That was nice. His body was nice, smooth and wet along the back. She ran her hands there. She lifted her legs. He groaned deep in his throat and the thrusts came faster.

So did the glass banging against the wall. She shot an annoyed look at the headboard. How could he concentrate on anything with that noise? she wondered.

"Put your legs around my waist," he moaned into her ear. She did, though they slipped a little on his sweaty skin.

He stopped for a moment and Anna almost said something about the glass but didn't, figuring this one was for him. That was fine. A little disappointing, but fine. Sam got up on his knees, lifting her hips up onto his thighs, her legs over his elbows.

Well, hello, her body murmured with renewed interest. But as soon as he started moving, the glass began its thumping and the sensations she was feeling died. It was hopeless, really.

"Sam," she started, her voice loud and practical in the room.

Sam reared back and roared, furious in the moonlight. He leaned forward, driving hard into Anna, harder and deeper than anything in her life and she gasped. He lifted his arm and with one long violent sweep of his hand, cleared the headboard of all the glass, shattering it with spectacular noise on the far wall.

There was a moment of stunned silence while she stared up at him with surprise and with a long slow shudder her body woke up and began cheering.

I'm back! Her body screamed and there were fireworks and electric pulses deep in the muscles that were embracing him.

The fires were back and the *nice* tingles that she had felt earlier flashed into need. Blistering and sudden.

She pushed herself up, his erection deep and going deeper. She gripped his hair, pressed her breasts against his chest and bit his lips.

"Come on," she breathed fiercely into his mouth.

He laughed, deep and dark and her body clenched hard around him in helpless response. With another roar and the same barely controlled violence, Sam and Anna proceeded to tear the room apart.

Anna's body, after all, had long years to make up for.

12

SAM WATCHED Anna sleep. She was a gorgeous woman, fantastic in the throes of the sex they just had, lovely in shorts, perfect with her hair up and her neck on display, but she was one ugly sleeper.

He smiled and tried to tip her chin up so her mouth wouldn't gape open in that way. She just shook him off and went back to her heavy, openmouthed breathing. Not quite a snore but not quite silent, either. Sam didn't care. After the things she had done to him, for him, with him, she could breathe however she wanted.

The moonlight came into the very white, stark room. He understood a little why she wouldn't think of decorating a place, having moved as much as she had when she was a kid. But she had been in this apartment six years. Sam thought about painting a canvas green and giving it to her. Art. She would love that. She would laugh like a loon and Sam would be forced to strip her naked and do dirty things to her.

She had a strange appetite for dirty.

He looked past her at the far wall and the glass shards that glittered in the shadowy light. He looked back at Anna, now drooling *and* breathing heavy and wondered how lucky a man could get.

He smoothed out some of her hair, blue-black against the white pillowcases and silky against his hands. For the past year his mind had been trained not to think beyond the next day. A day at a time of his useless life was all he could handle. But suddenly he realized that tomorrow wasn't enough.

Not nearly enough. He took a deep breath and tried to imagine next week. He pressed against the boundaries he had set up after his accident. His narrow world that he had grown used to. He imagined the week after next. Anna's heavy-breathing presence beside him strung his days together in a way that wasn't just bearable, but good. Good in a way that made him anticipate the days ahead.

He knew her plan—the six-month deal—and he guessed if things lasted that long, he might be able to balance out her life. Work and play in equal parts. The only problem was, how was Sam going to equal out his own life?

Johnny's suggestion about a position at the firehouse rang in his head.

"Sam?" Anna croaked. Sam looked down and smiled, her voice had to be about gone. He should have known the dirty librarian was a screamer. "What's wrong?" she whispered, her blue eyes limpid in the night.

"Nothing," he breathed and brushed his thumb across her forehead, down her cheek, across her lips, which opened and her tongue came out to touch the tip of this finger. Her eyes were on his in the hushed darkness of her bedroom and it was pretty much the most erotic thing he had ever seen or experienced.

"Roll over," he told her firmly because he knew she loved that.

"Roll...?"

"Over." He helped her because she was a little slow, tangled in sheets and some of his clothes and because he was suddenly dying for her. He eased into her, nearly brought to tears by her body's warm welcome, by the beauty of her skin, by the things he felt slowly growing deep in his chest.

"SAM," ANNA LAUGHED soundlessly. Her voice was totally gone. He nuzzled her ear unable to stop touching her. Through the window the sky was growing lighter, gray and pink a bit, with yellow at the top corner. The new day was starting and Sam loved that. Really loved it.

"We need water," Anna told him pushing him away. "I'm dying and you broke my water glass."

"Smashed it," he said into her neck.

"Sam," she said and he looked into her eyes and would have done anything she asked.

"I'll get it," he breathed, kissed her nose and got out of the bed.

"Sam?" she said from the bed and he turned. "You've got a great ass."

Sam dived back into bed. Water could wait.

ANNA, WEARING Sam's T-shirt, came back in the room with a large plastic cup of water, a bag of oranges and peanut butter cups.

"What's the deal with you and oranges and peanut butter cups?" he asked, having noticed that was almost all she had in her kitchen. For a woman who ate like a maniac whenever he was around, she had a strange diet behind her own closed doors.

She smiled and looked down at the bag in her hand. "I read somewhere that if you had to live on only two things, you could get most of the vital nutrients you need from oranges and peanut butter. When we were broke that's what we ate. When I got a job I added chocolate because—" she smiled and shrugged "—I could. I just never got out of the habit."

"Breakfast of champions," Sam muttered hiking himself up higher on the bed. The sun was coming in in spades, heating up the room and bouncing off all the white. It kind of hurt to open his eyes. "You should paint this room."

"Hmm," Anna hummed stepping onto the bed, "I thought of painting it brown."

"Brown?" He looked around the small little room. It sure would make it darker. Sexier, sort of. "I'll help you."

She blinked at him. "Okay." She dropped the oranges in his lap.

"Ooof."

She set the cup on the shelf on the headboard and shot him an arch look. "I can't make any promises," he laughed leaning forward to bite her shoulder.

"Enough, enough. I need sustenance," she said, her voice a husky groan that, if Sam hadn't been all worn out and sore, would have turned him on.

He looked at his watch. "We should go get lunch." He began to peel an orange. Anna leaned over and licked the juice that sprayed his neck and at the touch of her tongue, Sam began to feel a little less sore. *My God, this is nuts*, he thought. Though he wasn't complaining.

"What time is it?" she murmured unwrapping a peanut butter cup.

"One." He was glad he had his VCR programmed to record.

Anna looked up, her eyes wide, her mouth open. "Uhh..."

"What's wrong?" he asked. It wasn't as if she had anything to do.

"I...ah... Look, don't make fun."

"I won't, Anna, what's wrong?"

"Let's move this little picnic to the couch."

"Why?"

"I've got to see what happens when Hunter's evil long-lost twin shows up."

"*The Palisades?*" Sam asked, having started to watch the same stupid show when he was laid up. He never missed an episode thanks to his trusty VCR.

"You, too?" she asked.

"Let's go." He grabbed the water and the oranges while

she grabbed the chocolates and the blanket. They curled up together on the couch to watch the show that neither of them were addicted to.

THEY ORDERED in some Chinese food, which got cold when Sam got distracted by Anna's long legs. But they ate it cold and Sam tried to work on his own game plan. Now that he and Anna had made love, he planned on keeping it as a regular occurrence in his life.

Keeping her in his bed—or him in her bed as it were—was going to take the same kind of tactics that it had taken to get her there in the first place. Let it become her idea, then he couldn't be accused of pushing her. *So far*, he thought looking at her lick soy sauce off her hand, *it's* worked like a charm.

Sam scratched his chest. He needed to shower. She needed to shower. They were covered in soy sauce and orange juice to say nothing of the dried sweat. Her hair was sort of standing on end, he tilted his head to try and see the back of it where it looked like a bird had made a nest.

"You have to hand that to me," Anna said, snapping him out of his study of the beautiful black tangle of her hair.

"What?"

"The fortune cookie." She pointed and he followed her finger to the plastic wrapped fortune cookie that was practically in her lap on top of the blue blanket they were sharing. "You have to hand it to me."

"Is your hand broken?" he asked, picking up the cookie and trying to balance it on her head.

"The fortune won't come true if you pick it up. It has to be handed to you." She picked up the other cookie and handed it to him. He took it and rolled his eyes at her.

"We're not dealing with ancient Chinese psychics. They print these things down on 14th Street."

"Still," she protested and Sam couldn't believe that she

was superstitious about this. She cracked open her cookie and ate the whole thing before reading the fortune.

She groaned and flopped back dramatically on the couch. "You're right," she said. "It's all a cruel sham."

He plucked the fortune out of her hand.

"You love Chinese food," he read, chuckling. "Well, it's hard to miss with that."

"Read yours," she insisted, her superstition apparently undaunted. He was completely taken with this Anna, too, this sort of childish Anna. Between the dirty librarian and this, he was a goner. He could feel it.

He cracked open the cookie, ate it all first before reading it as she insisted.

All you want is within your grasp, it said. Sam felt the hair on the back of his neck stand up.

"What's it say?" Anna asked, smiling. He thought about telling her, about letting her try to laugh it off after the day they'd had. But he didn't want the time they spent together to end in some sort of serious discussion about her life and her job and how she didn't want to have a relationship.

"It's says I am going to get lucky." He looked at her with his eyes wide. "These guys are for real."

"Come on." She tried to reach for it and he held it behind his head so she had to climb a little on top of him to try to reach for it. "Be serious."

"I am being serious, it says I am going to get lucky." He reached his hand under the T-shirt she had put on and let his hands wander all over her soft warm skin, until she wasn't reaching for the fortune anymore. "Very, very lucky."

He let the slip of paper fall out of his hand and he concentrated on everything he wanted that was within his grasp.

"ANNA, IT'S NIGHTTIME." Sam looked out the bedroom window where it was getting dark. "I have got to go." He breathed a kiss into her hair and started to pull himself away from her. She kissed his shoulder and leaned away and grimaced as their skin slowly tore away from each other like tape on tape.

"We are so gross," she breathed, rubbing the red strip of skin across her breast where it had pressed against his chest.

"Yep," he agreed. He was going to go home and shower and then he was going to go down to the firehouse. Or at least he was planning on it. The emotional hurdles between himself and his former place of work seemed much smaller from his position on Anna's bed.

In his cool dark apartment, surrounded by his cool dark life, there was no telling how high those hurdles would seem. How insurmountable.

But the day he had spent with Anna, laughing and having sex had given him a little foolhardy courage. Enough that he could consider going to the fire hall—he could think about it and picture himself doing it without feeling like every breath was being squeezed out of his body.

Everything you want is within your grasp.

"What's next in Operation Get Anna Her Job Back?" he asked, casually, pulling on his pants and T-shirt. When she didn't answer he looked over at her.

Shit, he thought. *Way to go idiot.* Anna was leaning back against the headboard, staring blindly into the middle distance like a woman who had lost something and was trying to remember where she put it. As he watched he could see the wheels turning and the floodgates closing and her withdrawing from him.

She fumbled on her bedside table for her glasses.

"Give me a call," he said breezily, but leaned across the bed to kiss her mouth slowly, loving the way her full lips seemed to cling to his.

"Right," she said, sort of sharply and Sam cursed himself again as he left the room, walked through her dark kitchen and out her front door.

ANNA KEPT HERSELF BUSY. Frantically, so. She showered, she stripped her bed and put on new sheets. She cleaned up the wreckage of the Chinese food, grabbing chopsticks and fortunes with careless and worried disregard.

She tried not to consider the past twenty-four hours of her life as a mistake. She tried to keep her perspective, but she was no dummy. That hadn't been just the most ridiculous sex of her life, that hadn't been the perfect fulfillment of some of her darkest and deepest fantasies.

That had been a beginning. She saw it in Sam's eyes, tasted it in his mouth. He wanted more. More of the same and more of things that she hadn't even considered in years.

Anna swept and mopped her floors and wondered if she had more to give him. She smiled as the mop stilled in her hands. She might. She just might.

The doorbell rang and Anna took a deep breath, preparing herself for Sam. Preparing a little speech about sex and perspective and the future and what she really wanted in this life. About going slow and priorities, but her heart was racing, beating hard in her chest. He had been gone for an hour and she missed him.

She flung open the door with a grin. "You couldn't stay—"

It wasn't Sam, it was Aurora Milan, nearly vibrating with angry energy.

She shoved a vase filled with half-dead roses at Anna and she dropped her mop in order to grab the fragrant red flowers.

"I found those yesterday in my broom closet at work! So, I called Arsenal and I can't get a straight answer from those people! What the hell do those mean?" Aurora cried, she rubbed a hand over her close-shaved head, her silver rings catching the moonlight. "Anna? Roses? What the hell is going on?"

For one sharp moment, Anna thought the top of her head might explode. She tried frantically to switch gears. She had opened the door expecting to find Sam and, instead, it was her life. Aurora. Goddess. Her whole life. Anna's priorities settled back around her like a familiar suit. A suit she had made. "Come on in, Aurora." Anna gestured into her apartment. Aurora, smelling like patchouli and radiating anger, walked into her apartment and Anna shut the door behind her.

SAM PARKED HIS CAR across the street from the firehouse at the corner of Leavenworth and Jackson. He hadn't been back here in a year. He looked around noting the changes in the run-down neighborhood that he loved. He had worked here for close to ten years and he had worked with a lot of the men inside the old building for just as long.

It was eight o'clock and the lights were on in the kitchen of the station. He could see men moving around up there. Doing dishes after dinner, Sam guessed and he almost heard them. Joe would be giving Tony a hard time over the meal and Eddie would be laughing as he dried the dishes, his laugh like a gong. Dave would be making coffee, talking about how bad he wanted a little cheesecake, that the diet his wife had put him on was killing him.

And Johnny...

Sam watched the short, fat man come out of the garage and sit down on the bench alongside the building. He lit up his after dinner cigarette, the only cigarette he would have all day after years of chain-smoking. He stretched his arms out behind him, tilted his head back and blew smoke rings in the dark night.

As though he was walking into a house already on fire, Sam didn't give himself a chance to think about what he was doing. He just did it. He opened his car door, stepped out and slammed the door behind him.

Johnny looked over at the sound and slowly, as Sam walked over to him, sat up. Sam got closer and Johnny stood.

He reached out his hand for a shake and Sam grabbed it, felt the tug as Johnny pulled him closer, up onto the cement landing. The light from the garage cut Johnny's face in half. His mouth and nose in the bright light, his eyes lost in the darkness.

"Hey, Johnny," Sam breathed, the bands of pressure around his chest making it hard for him to fill his lungs, making it hard for him stand up, making it hard to continue to keep blinking back the tears that were in his eyes.

Johnny smiled. "Hey, Sam," he drawled. He took a drag of his cigarette and then tilted his head back. "Boys," he shouted up to the open window of the kitchen. "Someone here to see you."

Sam kept his eyes on the ground. He kicked a pebble off the cement landing with his worn running shoe. A dim prayer filled the back of his head, a small voice asking for help and guidance in the next few moments.

Don't let me cry in front of these men, he thought and cleared his throat. He gasped for breath. Wished he was someplace else.

A voice from above them shouted out the window. "Who you got there, Johnny?" Sam could feel the eyes on the top of his head. He thought of Anna, of her drive and energy and will. Her face in the moonlight. Sam made himself look up.

"Hey, Eddie," he called out softly to the young, handsome Hispanic man hanging out the window.

"Holy shit." Eddie turned back around. "It's Sam," he said to the men behind him. Sam could hear their voices and the sounds of their feet as they made their way down the stairs toward him. Dave didn't bother with the stairs, he took the pole and ran toward Sam.

Sam braced himself, tried to smile and blink back tears at the same time.

"Hey, boys," he said and they were upon him. Hugging him, slapping his back. Dave gripped his hand with enough strength to break his fingers and Sam relished the pain. Relished the sound of their voices in his ears. The smell of Mike's spaghetti sauce was on all of them. A smile on every familiar and beloved face.

"Sammy boy, we missed you." It was Eddie, his round face shiny from the steam of the hot water upstairs.

"I missed you, too, guys." He scarcely managed to get the words out. "I missed you, too." Dave coughed, looking into the streetlight, blinking. Some of the other guys had a telltale shine to their own eyes. He couldn't believe it. He was such a fool for staying away so long.

"Anybody see the A's last night?" he asked and the men broke into a familiar and masculine chorus about baseball while they led Sam back inside.

"YOU'VE BEEN WHAT?" Aurora asked. She leaned forward across Anna's kitchen table. Pushing the mugs of tea out of the way. She grabbed Anna's hands in hers. "Tell me you're just joking with me."

Anna swallowed a laugh. Those were familiar words. It seemed like just yesterday she had been begging Camilla for the same thing.

"Aurora." Anna felt the myriad of silver rings the woman wore dig into her skin. "I'll be back in five months. It's not the end of the world." But the words stuck in Anna's throat and when Aurora's eyes narrowed, Anna knew she hadn't convinced the canny woman of anything.

Aurora's hazel eyes stood out against her very tan skin and Anna fought the urge to squirm.

"I agreed to go with Arsenal because of you, Anna," Aurora told her and Anna's stomach pitched. "I don't like this Andrew guy. I like you."

The words were simple and seemed somehow childish, but Anna knew that the woman made huge decisions based on things that uncomplicated. Aurora didn't travel on even numbered days. She didn't hire women whose names started with *L,* because she knew a girl named Lucy once that had died in a fire. She didn't eat anything with a face.

These were hard and fast rules. Daisies were good and roses were bad because roses were flowers you sent when someone died. It was that elementary to the woman.

Her idiosyncrasies made working with her like trying to work with a kindergartner.

"I'm not going anywhere, I am still at Arsenal."

"Not when I need you," Aurora insisted a little frantically and Anna couldn't argue. "This is the fall line we're talking about here." She took a deep breath. She got down on the floor and pulled her thin purple spandex-covered legs into the lotus position. "I can't work this way," she said between deep breaths, her eyes closed.

"Andrew is very good and Camilla..."

Aurora opened one eye. "Camilla sent me roses."

Anna pressed fingers to her temple and the ache that was drilling into her head. "It's going to work out, really."

"How? How is going to work out?" Aurora stretched her arms out, resting her wrists up on her knees. "You tell me how you are going to fix this." She started to hum.

"It's not broken," Anna insisted.

Apparently, it was the wrong thing to say because Aurora stood up in one tall, thin wave. "Well, it will be if you aren't back working on Goddess by Monday. Do you understand that?"

Anna could only look blankly at Aurora.

"I know you like to pretend that I am nuts, that my thoughts are silly. But this is business." Aurora narrowed her eyes and looked so painfully serious that Anna stood up to face her. "And in business you don't get the rewards unless you do the work. Do the work, Anna. Do the work *you* promised *you* would do."

That little grenade exploded inside of Anna and the silence in the room was deafening. *Do the work. Do the work.* The image of her mother, asleep on the couch, being fired or quitting every job she ever had. *Do the work.* What else did Anna have, but her work? She had started to believe in what Marie had said, that she didn't have anything more to prove. But Marie was wrong. Proving herself was a constant battle.

"Okay," Anna said with confidence she did not feel. Confidence that was a million miles away from her.

Aurora didn't say another word as she left, the door slamming behind her. Anna collapsed back into her chair wondering what in the world she was going to do.

13

ANNA BREATHED in through her nose, out through her mouth. Again, deeper and felt herself getting light-headed. She opened one eye just a little bit to see if anybody else looked as though they were going to pass out.

Or if anybody else was in serious pain.

Sitting cross-legged with an erect and elongated spine for ten minutes was excruciating. She scanned the room with her one partly opened eye for the teacher, Verna—a thin, supple woman of an indiscriminate age whose soft voice hid the temperament of a prison warden.

Not seeing the woman Anna took the opportunity to slump.

"Ah, ah," the teacher said from behind her. "Open up that chest, feel your breath." She touched Anna's shoulder lightly and Anna's shoulders snapped back up. Anna rolled her eyes underneath her closed lids. Marie had tried to tell her that going to a third yoga class really would make her like it, but the reality was that nothing was going to make Anna like yoga. Or Verna.

"Just empty your mind, get rid of all your concerns...." the woman was saying. Anna heard her voice retreating and she opened her eye up again. Verna was walking past Marie, who, while Anna watched, opened up one eye and managed to smirk at Anna. Anna stuck out her tongue and slumped some more.

Anna hated yoga.

Emptying her mind was the last thing she needed to be doing. Happy that Verna couldn't see into her skull, Anna went over her options.

"Anna," Verna called softly from across the room. "Chest open."

Anna's shoulders snapped back—again. Verna led them into another deceptively torturous position. With her butt in the air, Anna pressed back with her heels and leaned forward with the palms of her hands against the mat, trying with zero success to straighten her legs. Anna started work on the only two choices she had in the Aurora and Arsenal dilemma.

She could tell Camilla what was going on or keep it from Camilla and try to somehow get between Andrew Boyer and Aurora, running interference for the company she considered home. The company that was her future.

Anna's arms started to shake with the strain of holding herself up in what really was not a natural pose. Perhaps for dogs with some desire to face downward, but not for humans. Not for her. Anna looked over at Marie whose arms weren't shaking at all.

Stupid Marie. Stupid yoga. Stupid incense that was making her want to sneeze.

Anna tried to ignore the pain in her arms. Should she tell Camilla about Aurora's little visit, she was sure Camilla would tell Anna not to worry. But Goddess was not Camilla's baby. It was hers.

Verna asked them to *flow* down to their mats. Anna gladly collapsed. But the reprieve was not long lasting. Upward Facing Dog was just as punishing as the downward one. Anna gave it her best shot—mostly because Marie was watching and Verna was standing right behind her.

Instead of breathing through the pain—which was frankly the stupidest thing she had ever heard—Anna focused again on Camilla. Who, after telling Anna not to worry, would send Aurora more of the wrong flower and Aurora would yank Goddess from the company and Arsenal's future, as Anna saw it, would be in jeopardy. Some of their biggest clients had already been around for an unprecedented period of time. When they moved on—and they would move on because nobody stayed forever—Goddess would no longer be in the picture to provide the secure future Arsenal needed.

Anna took a breath and then another. She tried to think of the pros of telling Camilla about Aurora. It was logical. It was the right thing to do. Other than those fairly unconvincing arguments, nothing. No good would come of telling Camilla about Aurora.

Again Verna invited them to flow down to the mat. Anna collapsed this time with a very loud, "Ooompf."

With her face pressed to the mat Anna considered the pros and cons of running interference between Aurora and Arsenal.

Aurora would be happy. If she could convince Andrew to keep his mouth shut, which she was sure she could do, Camilla would still think Anna was on sabbatical. In essence, Camilla would be happy.

Anna would be happy because the company would be saved. Everyone would be happy.

The cons, of course, would be the out-and-out lying to her friend and mentor. The deception. *Tough call.* But she had to wonder that if she did everything right, how would Camilla ever know?

Anna pressed her hands under her chin and arched her back up. Did she really have the courage to do this? If Camilla did find out, Anna had no idea what Camilla would do. Part of her didn't want to believe that Camilla would actually fire her. But the rest of her had believed Camilla when she had laid down that threat.

For the remainder of the hour-long yoga class Anna hemmed and hawed between her two options and when she walked out of the studio, she was sweaty, sore and far from peaceful.

"What's wrong with you?" Marie asked, catching up with Anna outside of the studio. "Slow down!" Marie grabbed her elbow and Anna stopped walking. She took a deep breath and coughed. Jeez, yoga hurt. "What's the rush, Anna?"

"Sorry." Anna tightened her lips in what might look like a smile. "I've just got some stuff on my mind."

"What?" Marie asked, she opened up her drawstring backpack and stuffed her rolled-up, hot pink yoga mat into it.

"What?" Anna repeated dully. She quickly tallied up the pros and cons of telling Marie about Aurora and what she was thinking about doing. She decided against it. Marie's loose lips had sunk a million of Anna's ships over the years. She couldn't be trusted with this kind of stuff.

"Is it Sam?" Marie asked with waggling brows. She looked like a female Groucho Marx and Anna had to smile.

"Sure," Anna said. "I mean, yes, of course." Sam. Oh, God. It wasn't that she hadn't been thinking of him, it was just that she had been thinking of Aurora and Camilla more. But that was all right. That was the way it was supposed to be. Six months of smoke and mirrors and then back to the real life. Anna looked down at her tennis shoes for a moment as the thought of Sam washed over her. Scenes from the other night played through her memory like a pornographic film.

"Ohhhh," cooed Marie. "I like the looks of that smile. How about you buy me a coffee and tell me all about it."

"No," Anna hedged. Oh, she *wanted* to spill every little detail. She wanted to relive the graphic perfection of the twenty-four-hour sex-a-thon with the talented Mr. Drynan.

"I'll buy you coffee," Marie said, twisting the screws.

"I'm so gross." Anna gestured down to her sweatpants

and sweat-soaked T-shirt—two of the dumbest things to wear to a yoga class.

"So am I, who cares?" Marie gestured down at her flawless little black yoga ensemble and Anna scoffed. Anna looked like a high school PE teacher and Marie looked like an ad for Goddess.

"Come on." Marie put her hand through Anna's arm. "I just need one detail, one tiny detail, Anna. Have I ever asked for so little?" Marie's eyes were shining and Anna couldn't help but succumb. She wanted to brag so badly to her younger, wilder sister.

A FEW HOURS LATER, freshly showered and dressed in a clean pair of sweatpants, a tank top and her fancy, yellow flip-flops, Anna sat at her kitchen table with her pro and con lists in front of her. They were carefully numerated and color-coded, and while all signs pointed her toward running interference, she was still grappling with the idea of lying to Camilla. This wasn't passing off a fake boyfriend, this was real deception.

The phone rang, startling her from her thoughts of corporate espionage and she reached over to pick it up.

"Hello," she murmured into the phone, distracted by her pro and con list.

"Good morning, Anna." Anna's eyes snapped up and she pulled her legal pad into her lap as if Camilla, across the phone wire, could see her. "What are you up to?" Camilla asked in dulcet tones that had Anna cringing against the guilt that flooded her.

Tell her, tell her her conscience chanted.

"Ah, nothing," she said in a completely unconvincing way.

"Wonderful, that's just what you should be doing," Camilla said. The guilt felt like it was choking her.

Just open your mouth, tell her and she'll take care of it. Trust her. Just trust her to take care of it.

But that was the problem. Anna didn't trust anyone as much as she trusted herself. In the end, she would have to do it herself.

"What are you up to?' Anna asked in what sounded like a strangled voice to her own ears.

"I am just wondering if you and Sam would like to join us tonight for dinner at Sobo's. We have reservations at eight."

"I'll call him, but I think that would be fine," Anna said and Camilla blathered on a little bit about how wonderful Anna's sabbatical seemed to be going. Especially with Sam. And wasn't it wonderful that...

"I need to go, Camilla," Anna finally said, cutting off her boss.

"Of course, we'll see you tonight. Just call if there's a problem."

"You bet," Anna agreed and hung up the phone. She pressed her head to the receiver, her lips to the small holes of the mouth piece and knew the decision, for better or worse, had been made.

She took a deep breath. She called Sam and left a message on his machine about the dinner reservations, asking him to call her cell phone if there was a problem and, if not, to meet her at her house at seven.

"I..." She fluttered the edge of the pad with her finger and smiled a little thinking about Sam and what might happen after dinner. "I'm looking forward to seeing you again."

She hung up and went into her bedroom to consult her wardrobe for appropriate espionage attire.

ANNA DECIDED that the best method for optimum success lay in the weakest link. In this case, Andrew Boyer. While she couldn't get into Arsenal's offices—she could get into Arsenal's annex offices—the Starbucks across the street. In her previous attempts, she hadn't seen Andrew leave Arsenal. But today she intended to stay until he came out—regardless of how long it took.

She got there at noon dressed in her blue jeans, black T-shirt, a baseball cap Sam had left in her car and a pair of sunglasses. She chose her stakeout table, behind a rack of mugs but with a good view of the door. Perfect. All she needed was Andrew Boyer and a bladder of steel.

Finally at 3:00 p.m. after two lattes, a cup of tea and four different kinds of scones, Andrew walked in. For a moment, Anna couldn't believe it was him. Andrew looked awful. His normally pale complexion was absolutely sallow as though he had been living in a cave or something. The circles under his eyes looked deep and dark. His clothes were wrinkled, his tie had a coffee stain on it and his hair was standing on end.

Andrew ran his fingers through his hair while he read the menu, tugging a bit on the long ends like he could pull it out and Anna recognized the look of a desperate man. The look of a man who had been going head to head with Aurora Milan.

It wasn't pretty.

Anna had a quick vision of herself a few months ago and wondered, panicked if she had looked that bad.

She snuck up behind Andrew as he ordered his coffee with two extra shots of espresso.

"I got it," she told the cashier and slid a five across the counter. Andrew jumped and whirled like a man on an electrical wire.

"Jeez," he breathed and then his eyes focused on her. She lifted her dark glasses. "Anna?" He leaned away from her, looking around quickly as though he might be caught doing something wrong. Which, should Camilla see him, could certainly be construed as such.

Anna took pity on him. "Come on." She grabbed his elbow

and his cup of straight caffeine and led him to her table behind the mugs.

"Anna what the hell are you doing here?" he asked. He flopped down wearily in the chair across for hers and grabbed his coffee, sucking it down in a few swallows. Anna watched him in amazement.

"You look awful, Andrew."

"Thanks, Anna," he mumbled sarcastically and Anna was even more appalled. Andrew was a seriously wounded man if the best he could come up with was "thanks, Anna." In their three-year battles over leftovers and dish duty and client priorities he had managed to come up with the most inventive insults she had ever heard. Even when she threatened his life with those chopsticks he had managed to tell her to go to hell with impressive creativity.

"Aurora Milan came to see me at home," she told him, deciding that a direct hit would be most effective. Andrew's eyes widened, then right in front of her he collapsed, thunking his head on the table.

"I can't do it, Anna," he said to his feet, rolling his head across the table. Anna looked around embarrassed. "I can't handle the woman, she's like—"

"A child?" Anna supplied. This was going better than she had even planned.

"Yes, she's completely—"

"Erratic, unpredictable?"

Andrew sat up, his face creased and sprinkled with crumbs from some of the scones she had had earlier. "I don't know what to do, Anna." He shrugged, shook his head.

Just what she needed. A helpless, broken Andrew.

Anna Simmons, top of the world.

Anna scooted her chair around to his, put a comforting hand on his shoulder. "I'll tell you what we're going to do..." She leaned close and in calm, cool tones, whispered her plan right into Andrew's willing ear.

ANNA COULD NOT believe the day she had had. Getting Andrew not only to agree to her plan—which in her own mind
had seemed fairly harebrained, but also to completely buy
into it, gave her an incredible buzz. She'd even seen some
color returning to his face, some spark in his muddy brown
eyes. His reaction had made her begin to see her plan as
more genius than harebrained. If Andrew could keep his
cool and his mouth shut, things would work out fine. He was
a good worker, he was just too young and inexperienced for
this project.

Andrew had been worried for a moment about the recognition that would all go to him when she had done all the
work and she could only stare at him.

"This is about keeping my client," she finally told him.
"You can have the recognition, I'll take Arsenal. And I want
Goddess there when I take it."

The power of saying those words, of meaning them and
being able to do something about the situation must have
gone to her head, because there was no other explanation for
having gone over to Marie's house afterward. The result was
yet another "New Anna."

Anna stood in front of her own dime store, full-length mirror and clapped a hand over her mouth before she could gig-
gle.

Sam was going to lose it.

Anna turned a little bit in the mirror. The past few weeks
of eating had given her a little flesh and Marie's purple dress
looked good. Anna's hair lay across her neck and shoulders
like a shiny blue-black cape and Marie's painful, yet sexy,
black sandals gave her height and—as Anna turned trying to
get a view of the back—made her butt look like...well, a butt.

She clapped her hands, feeling giddy and sexy and ready
for one Sam Drynan.

"Hello," she purred to her reflection. She grabbed the
glass of wine that Marie had insisted was an important part

of any date preparation. "Hello, Sam." She pursed her lips and took a sip of wine.

"Hello!" Sam's voice called out from the front of her apartment and Anna, startled out of her head, sprayed her reflection with the mouthful of white wine.

"Hi, Sam," she called out in a warbly, coughing voice that did not purr at all. "Just a second." She grabbed her pillow and wiped up the wine. She checked her reflection again and tried to regain her poise.

"You know, you can't just leave your door open like that," he shouted from her kitchen. She heard him open her fridge and take out one of the beers she had bought for him after leaving Marie's. "You're a single girl..." He continued to blabber on about safety while Anna heard him open her cupboards and pull out a glass.

He made himself at home. She closed her eyes, her hands pressed to her chest, and waited for the annoyance. It didn't come. Sam was here, in her house, going through her cupboards and she was only thrilled. She was wearing a sexy dress, uncomfortable shoes and something that didn't at all count as underwear.

He could go through all her cupboards. He could leave the seat up on the toilet.... Well, that might be a bit much. But she didn't care. He was here and they had forty-five minutes to kill before they had to get in the car to go to dinner.

Anna left her bedroom carrying her glass of wine.

"You don't have screens on your windows, either?" Sam was saying looking out her kitchen window. "Why don't you just invite the bad guys—" Sam turned and Anna tried to strike a moderately sexy pose against the doorframe while not falling over in her heels.

Sam's mouth fell open, then slowly lifted into one of those smiles Anna loved. One of those smiles that promised a million dark and dirty things.

"Hi, Sam," she said, surprised by the huskiness of her

voice. The dress, the pose, the wine—for a moment, Anna thought she might be channeling Sharon Stone.

"Hi, Anna," Sam murmured as he took the few steps across the black-and-white linoleum of her kitchen floor to stand in front of her. Close enough that she could feel the warmth of him. She took a deep breath and met his eyes.

"I see you already got something to drink…"

"Call Camilla and tell her we can't come," Sam said, his eyes hot and serious.

Anna blinked as certain parts of her body melted. She took a deep breath and Sam watched her chest encased in the tight purple fabric and his eyes got hotter. Anna felt flooded with a certain addictive confidence and power. Lust ran through her like a river.

"I don't think I can do that, Sam," she told him putting her wineglass down on the counter in case he was going to do something crazy like jump her right there against the wall.

Yeah, yeah! her body applauded.

"I think you had better do that, Anna." His hand slowly reached out to touch her, so slowly that Anna's breath vanished as she waited to see where that hand would land. So slowly that the whole night flashed before her eyes in excruciating detail.

His hand rested on her chest and his fingers settled on the small scrap of fabric between her breasts. Her breath was a shallow gasp and her eyelids felt weighted. He pulled her toward him, his eyes boring into hers. She resisted because that was sexy. Even sexier when his eyebrow kicked up as if asking her if that was the way she wanted it.

Anna swallowed and lifted her own newly replucked eyebrow in teasing response and there was a split second before his body came at her, pushing her up against the wall. His mouth was there. Her hands were there, pulling at the fine fabric of the blue shirt he was wearing. His big palms slid under the tight skirt of her dress.

He suddenly pulled back, his hands hot, squeezing the flesh of her hips. "Are you naked under that dress?" he asked, his voice throttled. He pressed a kiss to the skin of her shoulder.

"Not—" she gasped when the kiss turned into a bite "—quite."

An hour later Anna finally called Camilla and told her that Sam had suddenly gotten very sick. Sam needed to stay in bed.

14

"SEE?" SAM SAID, turning around to face Anna as she struggled up the same hill Sam had nearly run up. The man was in crazy good shape. "I told you it was beautiful."

Anna reached the top and bent over with her hands at her waist, trying desperately to get her breath back.

"Very...nice," she panted.

Golden Gate State Park was filled with people, as was usual on a Sunday. They had hiked through fields of nappers and readers and lovers on blankets. Sam led them through an impromptu soccer match, past the museum, up to "the perfect spot." A large green field with a view of the water and about half the number of people in other parts of the park.

Seagulls squawked and Anna took great gulps of the salty sea air.

"You're not looking," Sam laughed and pulled the backpack off his shoulders.

"I...can't." And it was true. She felt as though her eyeballs were pounding in time with her heartbeat. She had to get to the gym more often. Yoga was not enough if she was going to be hanging out with Sam. Boot camp wouldn't be enough.

Sam continued to chat about this spot in the park and coming here with his father as he pulled out a bright red blanket and spread it on the grass. Anna happily collapsed onto it. She flung her arms wide and rolled gratefully onto her back. Sam leaned over her, his blond hair and green eyes spectacular against the white clouds and bright blue sky.

She smiled and cupped his cheek with her hand. "It's very beautiful," she told him and met him halfway when he leaned down to kiss her. It was chaste and sweet and as perfect as all the hot and heavy kisses.

"Hungry?" he asked.

"Always," she answered and he laughed. He started pulling out a picnic lunch that he had brought with them. "Burritos?" Anna asked, amazed. Did the man eat anything else?

"Not burritos," he insisted. Cold chicken, corn tortillas wrapped in foil, salsa, guacamole—Anna eyed him knowingly. "Looks like burritos to me."

He shrugged and started to dig in. Anna joined in without another thought. The food was delicious. He'd also brought along plenty of water and big, fat, ripe cherries.

After eating they lay back on blanket, Anna making a pillow out of Sam's shoulder as they watched the high clouds move, carried on wind they couldn't feel.

"I got a job," Sam said. Anna turned over to look him in the eye.

"What kind of job?" she asked, amazed and happy he had brought this up—Sam's work was a subject they never broached. Though the more time they spent together, the more she wanted to know. But she wasn't sure what the rules were, at what point things got too personal. It had felt too personal to ask about his work, so she hadn't. But she had a lousy gauge—talking about the weather sometimes seemed too personal to her.

"It's with the fire department." His hand curled around her neck and smoothed down her spine.

"But I thought...?"

"Yeah, those days are over for sure." He shot her a look that she couldn't quite read. Acceptance? Resolve? She wasn't sure, but it was different and she sensed that something had happened for Sam. A corner had been turned and he was better for it. She smiled, huge.

"So what are you doing?"

"Well, it's two part. I am a new regional coordinator for the Fire Safety program."

She winced and looked at his profile. "A desk job?" she asked softly, thinking that this big vibrant man was wasted behind a desk in an office somewhere.

"Some of the time," he admitted and shrugged. "It was inevitable, Anna. But—" he looked back up at the sky and smiled "—I do go to elementary schools teaching kids about fire safety. The other part of the job is at the Academy, teaching recruits."

"Perfect!" Anna cried. She rolled on top of him and pressed her face to his. "Sam, that's the perfect job for you. I can't believe it."

"I know," he whispered into her ear. "I know."

He reversed their positions so he was leaning over her. His hand slid up to her waist and started going higher. "You know what else is perfect?"

"No," she whispered coyly.

"Your breasts," he whispered and Anna shrieked as his hands slid under her pink T-shirt. "They are just perfect."

"Sam," she wiggled, trying to push his hands away, but she was laughing and not entirely sure she didn't want his hands there.

"Well, well, well," a voice murmured above them and Sam quickly rolled off Anna. There stood Camilla and Michael with a few of their grandkids. The grandkids were giggling behind their hands. Anna, feeling as though her mom had caught her making out with her boyfriend—which had never happened—sat up, pushing her clothes down.

"Let's go, kids." Michael winked and led the kids away to a different part of the field.

Camilla stood there, a blanket folded in her arms, smiling knowingly as Anna and Sam coughed and cleared their throats and tried to arrange their clothes and stand up at the same time.

"No, no. You stay there. Glad to see you're feeling better, Sam," Camilla called over her shoulder as she walked toward her family and the camp they had set up a hundred yards away.

Anna and Sam sat in stunned silence. "Did you know...?" he asked, watching them walk away.

"I had no idea," Anna told him.

"That was lucky," he said and lay down, his hand tracing her spine, finding the gap between her shirt and pants and sliding under her shirt.

"Yeah," Anna agreed and lay down next to Sam. "It was."

They curled up together and napped. Sam told her nonsense and she laughed at it. He tried to grope her and she didn't fight him off too hard. And the whole time, one thought marched through the back of her mind.

I did it. I've got a life.

SAM ROLLED OVER and stretched out his hand for Anna only to encounter cool, empty sheets. He opened one eye. She wasn't there. He put his head back on the pillow and waited for her to return from the bathroom. After what seemed far too long, he rolled over onto his back and looked at his watch—3:30 in the morning.

"Anna?" he called out, his voice thick with sleep.

"I'm here," he heard her respond from another part of her apartment. He swung his legs out of bed and went to go find her. Oddly enough, at three-thirty he didn't want to wake up in her bed alone.

Anna was sitting at her kitchen table, her laptop open in front of her, casting a green light onto her face and into the otherwise completely dark apartment. "What are you doing?" He leaned against the doorjamb and rubbed his eyes. He yawned. "Searching for porn?"

She laughed and looked up. *Man, the shadows and light from the computer do weird things to her face. She looks so different.* "Come back to bed," he said.

"I'll be there in a second, Sam."

"I'll tuck you in," he cajoled.

She seemed to think it over for a moment, which was disconcerting in the middle of the night with a woman who was more unemployed than him. But then she closed her computer and the apartment was completely black except for the moonlight coming through the kitchen window.

"What were you doing?" he asked.

"Nothing. How about you let me tuck you in?" she asked and it sounded good to Sam.

SAM WAS PRETTY SURE he wasn't wrong. He checked his watch—5:00 p.m. He was completely sure he was supposed to meet Anna at her house at five so they could go out to eat with Camilla and Michael. It was Tuesday. It was five o'clock. Where was Anna?

He sat down on the steps and waited for her, hoping nothing had happened to her.

Twenty minutes later, Sam went back to his apartment to call her cell phone for the third time. Her message kicked on immediately. Her cell phone was turned off.

Sam tried not to panic. He took a few deep breaths. But, this was so not like his very organized Anna who chastised him for being five minutes late.

He looked out his living-room window and saw Anna trudging up the path.

"What in the...?" he muttered. She was dressed in a business suit and carrying her laptop. He continued to watch as she fished in her purse for her keys and must have caught sight of her watch. She clapped a hand to her forehead and turned and ran down the stairs toward his condo. He opened the door before she knocked.

"Oh, no, Sam I am so sorry...." she gasped. Her face was sincerely contrite, but he was still confused and a little peeved that she hadn't thought to call. That she had, it would appear, forgotten him.

"Anna, what were you doing?" he asked quietly. "I was worried."

She blinked at him for a moment, her face inscrutable and that sent the wheels in his own head turning. Then she smiled ruefully. "I know. I was helping Marie with some stuff with the bank for the restaurant and... I am so sorry, Sam."

She reached out and curved her hand around his bicep. It wasn't that he intended to hold some kind of grudge, but he just couldn't shake the feeling that something wasn't right. She pulled herself closer and rested her head against his chest for a moment.

"I am so sorry, Sam."

He blew out a breath. She was sorry. He was fine. They were going to be late for dinner.

"It's all right," he said and pressed a kiss to her head. "I'm starved. We should get going."

"No problem." She snapped her head back. "Let me go change." She moved to walk away and he grabbed her hand, following her out the door.

She turned and he locked the door. "I'll watch," he told her.

"Then we'll never get to dinner," she groaned. He urged her down the steps and across the lawn. They made it to dinner. Late and Anna had no underwear on, but they made it.

AFTER PLENTY of last kisses goodbye, Sam left for the meeting at the firehouse. Anna had grown used to Sam in the month they had known each other. She knew his sense of humor, his sex drive, his sometimes filthy mouth and mind, but this part of Sam, the man with a sense of purpose, was new. New and exciting. He walked a little taller; his eyes were a little lighter. He was infinitely, dangerously more attractive to Anna.

She shut the door behind him and leaned her forehead against it taking deep breaths to clear her mind. Calm her beating heart.

She turned around and found her laptop casting a shadow on her kitchen table. Work. The meeting yesterday with Aurora at Goddess's offices had gone very well. Aurora agreed to the subterfuge—anything to keep Anna in the picture, anything to keep roses out of the office.

Anna cringed thinking of the lie she'd told Sam. She had almost told him the truth about working for Goddess, but she knew he would disapprove. And she didn't want any disapproval marring what they had. Besides, Sam was smoke and mirrors. Arsenal was the stuff that lasted.

Do the work you promised to do.

She had helped Aurora create Goddess Sportswear. She had paved the road with her own blood, sweat and tears, but that road went both ways. Aurora and Goddess had created her, too.

It was a relationship that would carry Arsenal for years. It was the future. Anna was putting in the work now to make sure that future was strong and successful.

A few lies, a relationship with a man that was not going to last, a selfish but fleeting sense of…what…happiness? What did those measure against Arsenal, the work she had promised to do and the future?

In the end, nothing else mattered. People always leave and all Anna had was herself and what she could do.

Anna swallowed hard against the bitter taste in the back of her throat and pressed a hand to the ache in her stomach. She must be hungry. She took an orange out of the fridge and peeled it while she stood over her laptop. She really had some work to do.

Andrew had been e-mailing Anna all of the pertinent information he had for the fall line. The files were huge and all over the place.

Andrew lacked a certain focus of vision. Anna settled down at the computer to focus on her own vision.

She ate another orange and some peanut butter cups and some of Sam's leftover lasagna from last night, but the empty, hollow ache in her belly did not go away.

"YOU WANT TO GO TO THE BEACH?" Sam asked over the phone. It was Sunday and there was nothing better than going to the beach on a Sunday.

"The beach?" Anna repeated and he gathered from her voice she wasn't too keen.

"Yeah, you wear a bikini, I'll bring a Frisbee."

"Frisbee?"

"I promise I won't throw it at your head." Sam kicked back in his couch and listened to Anna laugh. "I'll swing by and grab you in a half an hour."

Her laughter trailed off. "Sam, can I take a rain check?"

"Sure, what's..."

"I'll come to your house tonight, we can watch that stupid movie..."

"*Rocky* is not stupid."

"Whatever, we can watch it later."

Sam hung up the phone and realized she hadn't said what she was doing.

"IT'S TWO O'CLOCK in the morning," Sam groaned into Anna's neck. "What are you doing awake?"

"I'm just thinking," she whispered.

"What are you thinking about?"

"Arsenal and Goddess," she told him. He lifted his head

from her neck and blinked at her suddenly feeling wide-
awake. "Isn't that against the rules?"

She shrugged. "I can't help it."

"I'VE GOT TO GO," Anna told Andrew for the twelfth time.
She started putting the files into her briefcase and closing
down her computer. If she left now and broke a million traffic laws she would get to Sam only ten minutes late for the
barbecue he was having at his condo for the guys in the fire
department.

"Anna." Andrew stopped her. "Ten minutes. We just
need ten more minutes, we're so close. Aurora asked for
these numbers tomorrow."

Anna looked around at the coffeehouse that had become
her home away from home for the past week. The scattered
papers, the empty coffee cups. A view of the bay and an uncomfortable couch and it could have been her office.

"What's going on with you Anna? This is work..."

"Fine, fine, fine," she muttered sitting back down, tired of
fighting Andrew, tired of fighting the voices in her head.
Tired of fighting the pull of Sam.

Something was going to have to give and she knew it
would never be Arsenal.

SOMETHING WAS GOING ON, Sam was sure of it. He paced outside the movie theater for another ten minutes. This had
been her idea. Hers! After being over an hour late to the barbecue he threw last week and breaking the date to ambush
Camilla and Michael at the Symphony in the Park on Saturday, she had said "let's go to a movie, just the two of us."

He had been happy to agree at the time, having long ago
gotten bored with the game they were playing with Camilla.
He knew an apology when he heard it. Especially from
Anna. The past two weeks she had been nothing but apolo-
gies.

She had cancelled the Saturday date and been late for two
others because of the problems Marie was having with the

bank. When he pressed about what kind of problems, Anna waved him off with some sort of vague answer or she got her hands down his pants. Either way, he had let it go.

But he was beginning to think that Anna was lying. She was throwing him a million mixed signals. He had had to cancel a dinner date last week because a training session at the academy had run long, but he had come over to her house later with takeout. He had spent the night and she had behaved as if nothing was wrong.

The other night she had arrived on his doorstep wearing a black overcoat and nothing else. That had been nice. But tonight she was flat-out standing him up.

"Mister? The show just started. You want a ticket?" the sixteen-year-old pimply kid asked from inside his ticket booth.

"No, thanks," Sam mumbled and stepped away from the bright lights of the theater into the darkness of the parking lot.

The problem here might not be with her, but with him.

He understood what their original agreement was, but at some point things had changed for him. He was in a different place looking at Anna with new eyes. He needed to know how she saw him before things went downhill any further.

He drove to Anna's apartment with a sickening combination of dread and anger in the pit of his stomach.

The lights were on in her living room, filtered through the light blue curtains she had bought when he had painted a few of her rooms two weeks ago. He turned off the car and watched her shadow lean across the table. Another shadow joined her and for a moment, Sam let himself think the worst. His hands clenched the wheel, but he knew that was just the easy way out.

He walked up the sidewalk, knocked on her door and waited, hoping that the right words would come to him, because right now he felt more than a little lost.

Anna opened the door wearing jeans, a T-shirt and her glasses.

"Hi, Sam," she said brightly, then he watched her remember where she had promised him she would be. Her face paled and her eyes closed. "Oh God, Sam," she breathed. "I'm so sorry."

The apology, as sincere as the last dozen she had made, should have soothed a little bit of the anger that was boiling inside of him. It didn't. It only seemed to make it worse.

"So you've said," he muttered. Anna's eyes popped open and he was unmoved by their sad, blue depths.

"Anna?" A woman's voice called from inside. "Everything okay?"

"Yes, I'll be..." Sam watched Anna get lost in hesitation. She turned partly toward him and then back toward the woman at the kitchen table.

"Umm." She bit her lip and took a deep breath. Sam stepped into her house past her. The woman at the table was wearing a loose fitting purple dress and a ton of silver jewelry. She smiled at Sam.

"Sam, this is Aurora Milan. Aurora, Sam." Anna made the introductions in a barely calm voice. He should have taken pity on her, on the strain she was obviously feeling, but he suddenly felt like the biggest idiot ever to walk the earth.

Helping Marie? Problems with the bank? Every excuse he had heard the past two weeks ran through his head. Every lie she told.

"Aurora from Goddess Sportswear?" he asked and Aurora nodded, smiling blankly. Sam started nodding, too. He turned toward Anna who looked pained and beautiful. He took a few deep breaths as he chewed his tongue.

Walk, man, he told himself. *Walk out the door and don't look back.*

Finally, unable to handle it any longer, he stormed past her out the door. He was halfway across the lawn before Anna caught up with him.

"Sam," she cried. "Sam stop, wait." He turned and watched Anna run across the lawn in her bare feet. The sight of her barefoot in the moonlight hit him in the gut and it all suddenly became painfully funny.

"I would hate for you to stop working on my account," he said sarcastically. She stopped in her tracks. "I mean, God forbid you ever stop working."

"Sam, I'm sorry..." she said stupidly and he closed the gap between them.

"Sorry for what, Anna?" he asked. "What exactly is making you feel bad right now?"

"I'm sorry that you're mad," she said softly. Sam shook his head in disbelief over his own gullibility. What a fool he was. "I'm sorry I didn't tell you about going back to work—"

"Are we done?" he asked, bitterly. Her beautiful face flinched and, for a moment, he was glad. "You have your job back. Apparently you met someone's criteria so you don't need me anymore, right?"

"I don't want things to be like this, Sam," she told him plainly.

"Me neither, Anna, trust me."

"Now that you know, can't we just go back to..." She lifted her hand and dropped it.

"To screwing?" Again she flinched a little, but her eyes met his straight on. It was ridiculous that a month and a half ago this conversation would have been a dream come true for him. This would have been exactly what he wanted. But he was a different man...because of her. He felt sick.

"It was never like that for me," she told him in a strong voice.

"Well, Anna, you're going to have to try and make it clear to me what I was," his voice was growing quieter. "Let's forget the lies you told me." He almost choked on the words.

"How about you tell me what's going on in your head. How about, for once, you tell me the truth and tell me what I mean to you."

"You're my friend."

Oh, my God! he thought. *That shit does hurt.* He pressed on. "Anna, you are not supposed to be working. You can't balance your life, you're lying and breaking dates and choosing work over everything else."

"Sam," she said on a sigh. Her eyes took flight, looking everywhere but at him and he knew what was coming. Tried to brace himself for it, but when the words came, they were more painful than he could have imagined. "We...ah. We had an agreement that this wasn't going to turn into anything serious."

It was all so awfully clear to him. *I'm in love with you. Sweetheart, I've been in love with you since I saw you dancing in the laundry room.* He couldn't stand here and listen to her tell him he meant nothing.

"You're right," he agreed as his heart broke into a million pieces. "So, let's end it now. You don't need me anymore."

"That's not true." Sam ignored her protest and thought about pressing a kiss to her forehead so he could feel her skin one more time, touch her hair. But in the end, he just turned around and walked over to his dark, empty apartment, pretending not to hear her voice behind him, calling him back.

15

"ANNA," MARIE SAID, her eyes filled with disappointment and anger. "Tell me you are going to go back to that good man on your hands and knees and beg—"

"Hell, no!" Anna shouted. She took another swig of her fruity Cosmopolitan.

"Hell. No. Jeez, Marie, no one goes around on their hands and knees anymore."

Do they? Anna wondered and looked down at her drink which she had spilled most of in her fervent defense of feminism. She lifted her T-shirt and sucked the booze out of the cotton. What was she defending? She looked at Marie, who was making more drinks, but she couldn't remember. She couldn't remember anything but the look in Sam's face telling her goodbye.

One whole week of staring out her window, hoping to catch him on his way back and forth to work and she hadn't been able to sight him. She'd left a hundred messages, which he didn't return. She woke up yesterday and some of her clothes that she had left at his house were stuffed in her mailbox.

He wasn't even giving her a chance to explain.

"Well." Marie tsked her tongue and poured more pink liquor into Anna's oversize martini glass and then hoisted herself back up into her seat. They were perched on Marie's ample counter in her orange kitchen. Despite the large and comfortable couch in the other room, they were having their sisterly heart-to-heart on uncomfortable, cheap Formica.

Which they had been doing since they were teenagers. "You should. You should be doing everything in your power to get that man back. There are two kinds of men in this world Anna, good ones and bad ones. And he was one of the good guys."

Anna's body, emboldened with whatever it was in these drinks, heartily agreed. And her heart, achy and confused, thought it was a good idea, too.

"Nope." Anna shook her head, perhaps a bit more than necessary, she thought when her hair got caught in the wrought-iron cupboard handle. "He's the one who ruined this."

Marie looked at her with openmouthed astonishment.

"You're joking, right?"

"No! Things were fine until he freaked out." Anna knew that wasn't true. She was lying again, pushing all the blame on to him. But in the end, what was the point? That crazy thing between them was going to end anyway. Now. Six months from now. Did it matter?

Yes. Yes, it does, her heart whimpered.

"Yeah." Marie put up her hand. "Let's go back to that. What'd he freak out about?"

Anna stretched across the counter and reached into the bag of grapes in the sink. "Don't you have anything other than fruit?" she asked. It was very unsatisfying to be drunk and eat fruit. "Something cheesy? Or fried?"

"No, you and I are on a diet."

"Oh." Anna put the grapes in her mouth.

"Why did Sam freak out?" Marie cried.

"Oh, right," Anna had forgotten why she was avoiding this topic. "Because Aurora was at my house and I had lied to him about working for Goddess." She looked down into her glass. Wow, those drinks went down fast. Anna looked up at Marie and realized what she had said.

Out loud. To her sister. "Don't tell Camilla."

"Anna." Marie hopped off the counter, her knees buckled a little but she recovered and came to stand in front of Anna. "I love you, I love you sometimes more than I can say. But you are an idiot."

"How many times do I have to say it, Marie? I am who I am. An affair with—" an amazing, wonderful, one of a kind man "—Sam, isn't going to change me."

"What about love, Anna? Wouldn't that change you?" Marie asked quietly.

Anna laughed. She laughed so hard tears came pouring from her eyes. "Marie." She put her hand on her sister's head. "You've watched *Pretty Woman* too many times. Life doesn't work out like that." Anna held up her empty glass. "More booze."

"Don't you think you've had enough?"

Anna checked. She still felt lousy. She still felt like crying. She felt the absence of Sam as if part of her body was gone. "Nope, not enough."

"This isn't going to make this better, you know?" Marie told her, pouring booze and juice into her cocktail shaker.

"Yeah, I know," Anna agreed and held out her glass for Marie to fill.

ANNA THREW HERSELF into Goddess. She ran Andrew into the ground. She even had Aurora begging for air.

"Anna?" Aurora asked from her lotus position on Anna's floor. "I need protein. I need Vitamin C." She laid down on the ground, putting her feet straight up onto the wall.

"There are oranges in the fridge. We can order in," Anna said without looking up from her computer screen. The numbers looked good, the sample magazine ads looked amazing, the press releases were clean and sharp and done. She had gotten the feedback from all of the focus groups who loved the fall line. Things were looking up, straight up. The fall line was going to put Arsenal on a whole new level. And

Arsenal, in turn, was going to make Goddess a household name.

"Anna, come on, take a break." Anna looked over at Aurora and was momentarily distracted by how easy she made that Downward Dog thing look.

"You go ahead." She turned back to her notes on the projected first quarter sales.

"This isn't good for you. You know that, right?" Aurora told her.

"So, I'm told," Anna said, scrolling through the information on her screen.

"I'll bring you something back," Aurora said, finally standing upright.

Anna nodded, far too busy concentrating on things that were possible. Things that were real and within her grasp.

Anna concentrated with all of her energy on the things that mattered.

THREE MONTHS through her sabbatical. One month after being dumped by Sam and two months after starting the Goddess fall line, Anna was done with it. She sent the final e-mail. Couriered the last zip drive. Approved the last color printout.

Aurora somehow had convinced Camilla to invite Anna to the reception-launch party being held in a week at Marie's new restaurant, which wasn't quite ready to be opened to the public, but was perfect for this sort of affair. Initially, Anna wasn't going to go. She had no interest in watching Andrew soak up the praise for her work. She had no interest in pretending to be rested and relaxed and uninvolved when she was sick with involvement. She was diseased with Arsenal and Goddess, feverish and nauseous.

She didn't want to answer any questions about Sam.

But she had nothing else to do and Marie had begged.

So she was going.

Anna slept for two days straight, bothered only by her increasing daytime television habit and an old recurring nightmare.

She was driving alone at night in an unfamiliar car down a very dark and deserted highway. For some reason it felt like the desert. It felt like Arizona, but having never been to Arizona, she couldn't be sure why she felt this way. But in her dream the darkness lurking outside of the car was the same darkness where her mother lived.

She was talking to Marie, who she knew was in the passenger seat, when something happened to a tire. An explosion and the car began swerving. Anna struggled with the car, with an effort that seemed superhuman. After getting the car to the side of the road, she looked to make sure her sister was okay, but her sister wasn't there. She wasn't in the back seat, either.

Anna got out of the car—upon waking she knew it was foolish to think her sister had disappeared, but in the grip of the dream it was very real and very frightening—and looked for her sister along the roadside. She couldn't find her. Car headlights came up over a hill in front of her and Anna stood in the middle of the road to flag the driver down. The car slowed down just enough that Anna could make out Sam's face as he drove by.

Anna woke up cold and dizzy. She wasn't dumb; she could read every not-so-subtle clue in the dream. There was just nothing she could do about it.

Between Anna's frenzied work on the Goddess campaign and her two-day sleeping jag, Anna's laundry had once again reached mammoth proportions. Since she didn't have the energy to baby-sit her own washer and dryer—tediously doing one load at a time—she was back in the complex's community laundry room.

Anna blindly put clothes in the washing machines. Colors,

whites, darks, she didn't notice. She was working on automatic pilot and even her automatic pilot was numb. She was forcing her mind to be blank. Thinking about Arsenal or Goddess was making her ill with ulcers and headaches, thinking about Sam felt worse. It felt as though she was running out of air to breathe.

So, she thought of nothing.

"Anna?" She turned slowly toward the door of the laundry room and the sound of the voice that she had forced herself not to imagine. The shadow being cast there was heartbreakingly big and tall and familiar.

"Sam," she said and she smiled, somehow relieved that he was there. She could breathe again.

"Hello." He stepped into the room, coming out of the shadows. He blinked a few times while his eyes adjusted to the light and Anna could only stare and grin foolishly.

He returned her smile quickly and then moved to one of the washing machines. He looked so good to her. He was wearing khaki pants and a blue polo shirt with the logo of the fire department embroidered into it. Gone was her nonchalant, aimless lover. This was a different man, restrained and purposeful.

"How are you, Sam?" she asked, her laundry forgotten.

"Good," he answered without looking at her. "Busy."

"How is work?" She took a few steps toward him, staring at his profile.

"It's good." He looked at her quickly out of the corner of his eye and she took another step closer. "How about you?" he asked, slamming down the lid on the machine. "How is work?"

The words weren't friendly and in fact, felt like a physical slap across the face. "I'm sorry," he breathed before she could say anything. His eyes traveled over her, looking, really looking at her for the first time since he'd walked in. She soaked up his attention.

"It's..." pointless, meaningless, nothing, the words rushed unbidden to her mouth from some part of her brain or maybe it was her heart speaking up. "Fine."

His eyes narrowed for a moment. "Are you all right?" he asked.

"Yes," she said quickly before other words could come running out of her mouth about how lonely she was, about the dream she was having, about the ache in her stomach.

"Anna, I don't..." He stopped and looked at his hands. Anna was suddenly overwhelmed by the memory of Sam telling her she was pretty. Beautiful. That she was amazing to him. Tears, burning hot and painful flooded her eyes. She looked away blinking furiously. "Please, don't take this the wrong way," he was saying. "But you don't look...well."

Anna laughed, a teary, wet, broken laugh.

"Are you pregnant?"

Her eyes flew to his. "No," she said quickly. A baby? The idea as foreign to her as the moon.

He sighed, obviously relieved. He nodded, seemed about to say something, then stopped. "Well..."

Anna could only blink at him as she tried to suck in air. "I miss you," she finally said.

Sam closed his eyes for a moment and Anna took a step closer to him, thinking perhaps he was weakening, perhaps she could reach him. She lifted a hand to touch him and he jerked away.

"Anna," he groaned. "I can't...do this. I can't be second place in a woman's life. I..." He shook his head, his face flushed with blood. "Goodbye, Anna," he said softly. He picked up his empty laundry basket and left.

That night Anna dreamed that it was Sam in the car with her, driving through the cold desert night. When the tire blew and she looked around for him, he wasn't there. This time the headlights over the far hill never came and she walked down that lonely Arizona highway all by herself.

16

MARIE WAS THROWING a beautiful party. The place looked great. The work Anna herself had put into hanging pictures and whatever the dumb thing was with paint and the plastic bag looked great. The whole room resembled a beautiful old marketplace with its wooden benches and tiled tables. The plants that Anna was sure would be dead in a matter of weeks, were currently alive and thriving. Candles and small lanterns were everywhere and the drinks were flowing. The laughter was a tad drunken in sound and the conversation had long ago stopped centering on the greatness of the combined Arsenal and Goddess forces as people mingled and chatted and ate every single piece of food Marie set out.

The food was amazing. The fall line was gorgeous. Arsenal was on top.

"Anna, I can't keep taking all the credit here," Andrew said as he sat down next to her at her table in a dark corner of the festive room. "I feel awful."

"Don't," Anna told him. She spun her water glass in small circles on the table. "You worked really hard."

"Not nearly as hard as you," he said as he stretched his legs out in front of him and drank from his beer. He looked like a man who wasn't uncomfortable with anything. He was happy taking the credit, as she had known he would be. As she always did, she had planned this perfectly.

"Nobody works as hard as I do," Anna told him over the edge of her glass before taking a sip of water.

"Amen to that."

"Camilla is coming," Anna told him. "It's probably best if people don't see us together."

"Right." Andrew stood. "Good thinking partner." He flashed another of his weasely grins at her and Anna decided she would stay another five minutes, then go home and seriously consider the appeal of becoming an alcoholic.

Anna watched Camilla stop Andrew and congratulate him for the hundredth time before coming over to sit with Anna.

"Have you tried this organic beer?" Camilla asked, looking down at her full pint glass. "It's awful."

"Aurora's idea," Anna laughed wearily. Aurora, hard to miss in a batik sarong, was leading a little breathing seminar in the middle of the room. "She seems to like it."

Camilla shook her head and pushed the beer away from her. She crossed her long bare legs and pulled her red silk shawl up over her shoulders as she perused the crowd. Anna slouched a little more in her once favorite gray suit that now was too tight across the butt.

That's what a sabbatical will get you. A fat butt.

"Great party."

"Yep." Anna ran her glass across the red and cream tiles of the table.

"Marie worked hard."

Anna nodded. "Yep."

"Where's Sam?" Camilla asked without breaking stride.

Anna shook her head.

"You guys fight?"

"You could say that." Anna sighed. She stood to leave. She had hit the end of her rope. Three months ago, walking out of Arsenal with her arms filled with oranges and peanut butter cups she had thought that her life could not get any worse. But tonight, at the very moment when her whole life should feel as fulfilled as possible, Anna had never felt worse.

"Well, it looks like he's here to make up." Anna's blood rushed to her feet and her skin awoke in a long rush of pins and needles.

"He's here?" she asked, stunned and rooted to the spot. Camilla stood behind her and pointed to where Sam was standing just inside the doorway, looking uncomfortable and gorgeous in a black suit jacket Anna had never seen him wear. He craned his neck looking around for someone.

Me, Anna thought. *He's looking for me.* She walked away from Camilla, unsure of what she was doing. Planless and scared, Anna walked toward Sam on legs that trembled.

A few feet away from him, just as she had thoughts of throwing herself down in front of him and begging for a second chance, her gorgeous sister—looking flushed and radiant—swooped from out of nowhere to greet him.

Anna watched as Marie kissed Sam's cheeks and her heart beat hard as Sam smiled fondly at her and slipped his arm around her shoulder, hugging her to his body.

All of the things Marie had said during Anna's relationship with Sam, about how he was one of the rare good guys and how Anna wouldn't know what to do with him, suddenly became a looped soundtrack to the scene she was watching.

Sam was laughing and Marie's lipstick was all over his cheek.

Things exploded inside Anna's head. Land mines that had been buried in Anna's youth detonated. Her mother leaving. Marie's constant and shameless appeal to the opposite sex. Her years of sleeping on the uncomfortable couch in Arsenal's office.

They all became a Fourth of July fireworks extravaganza in her head.

And she realized she couldn't sacrifice Sam the way she had sacrificed everything else in her life. Not for Arsenal. Not for her career and most definitely not for Marie. She wanted something for herself and that something had to be Sam. She was wasting away without him. She knew that now.

Anna marched over to her sister and the man she was suddenly prepared to do battle for. "Marie."

"Hey, Anna, glad to see you out of your dark corner."

Anna wrapped her hand around Marie's wrist and yanked. "Get lost." Marie held her ground, her eyes turning mutinous in a way that made Anna want to pull her hair.

"Hi...ah, Anna?" Sam said slowly, obviously catching on to what was transpiring between the sisters.

"Sam, please help yourself at the bar. I'll be back in a moment." Marie's eyes never left Anna's, but somehow she was able to send Sam toward the bar with a little pat on the back.

Anna saw red. "Sam, don't you dare leave," Anna told him with no pat on the back. He left, casting nervous backward glances the whole way. "You better have a good..." Anna stepped in toward her sister.

There was some microphone reverb and the music suddenly was turned down as Aurora got up to say a few words.

"Follow me," Marie said through clenched teeth and Anna followed her into the bathroom. The door shut behind them and Aurora's voice was muffled through the solid wood.

Marie turned, eyes narrowed, but Anna was ready for her. "What the hell do you think you're doing?" Anna shrieked.

"I'm not doing anything. I invited Sam to a party, big deal."

"Big deal?" Anna couldn't believe it. "Big deal!"

"Yeah, Anna." Marie crossed her arms over her red chef's jacket and leaned against one of the stalls in the small bathroom. "You're so busy creating your empire, I didn't think you would mind. Why? Do you mind?"

Mind? Anna's heart was being blown apart. Of course, she minded. Of course, she...

Marie quirked her perfect eyebrow and grinned.

Of course, she'd been had. Anna stepped past her sister and put her head against the cool metal of the stall. Marie turned, leaning on her side, and patted Anna's shoulder. There was some applause coming from the next room and Anna could hear Aurora laughing.

"You're so busy trying not to be Mom, that you're doing the exact same thing she did."

"No, I'm not." Anna lifted her head. She was prepared to admit a lot of things, but that wasn't one of them.

"Yes, Anna, you are. You're staying in one spot spinning around so hard that no one can get close to you. Instead of driving away yourself, you're driving everyone else away. It's you and no one else. Same as Mom."

Anna closed her eyes in defeat, imagining her mother driving away before anything got too hard, before she had to commit more than she wanted to. Marie was right. She drove Sam away, she made him leave. It wasn't his fault. He tried and gave as much as he could. He changed his life around and she couldn't tell herself that she didn't want to be a part of that. She did. She wanted anything he could give her.

"I think I love him," Anna breathed. "I mean, I'm pretty sure."

"Then you better go get him, because he is one pissed-off guy." Marie laughed. She leaned over the sink and fluffed up her hair in the mirror.

"Thanks, Marie." Anna caught Marie's eye in the mirror.

"Go, go."

Anna pulled open the door and the entire room filled with well-dressed and slightly drunk people gasped and turned toward her.

"There she is," Aurora was saying, her voice loud and shrill, "Anna take a bow." She smiled and shrugged, oblivious to the pained expressions of the people around her. "I couldn't keep it a secret any longer."

Anna searched out Andrew who was sitting at one of the small tables with his head in his hands. Defeated, again.

Shit, Anna thought. She caught Camilla's eye and the woman looked as though she was going to start spitting fire. But Anna had no time to deal with this particular catastrophe.

Sam was heading for the exit.

"Anna?" Aurora was prompting her in the silence.

"Sam!" Anna called out. Sam stopped for a moment, looked at her, burning her with his gaze. She wanted to tell him that she was sorry. That she was confused and hurt and that she wanted to be better. But he shook his head, then he opened the door and walked out. Anna started to follow.

"Anna?" It was Camilla behind her and the tone of the woman's voice—hard, angry and disappointed—made Anna stop. Mother and boss in one was a tough combination to walk away from. "Is this true? Did you do all this work?"

Anna watched Sam's blond head pass the front window. He was leaving. She was losing him and, suddenly, the decision was easy. Her heart led the way.

"Yeah," she told Camilla. "I did it. Fire me, but I've got to go." She took off in a run through the crowd of her colleagues who parted, startled by her exodus. She hit the door and launched herself into the warm night air.

"Sam!" she shouted after his retreating body. He was walking downhill, away from her. At the sound of her voice, he didn't even pause. Anna kicked off her heels, leaving them on the sidewalk and charged after him, shouting his name.

Finally, he turned, crossed his arms over his chest and waited for her.

She slowed down to a jog and then stopped a hand's breadth away from him. "Sam," she panted.

"Go back inside, Anna," he told her, his voice cold enough to give her goose bumps. "There's nothing for you out here." He started to walk away again, but Anna grabbed him with both hands and had no intention of letting him go.

He sighed. "Anna, what the hell do you want?"

"You," she breathed. Saying it made her feel better. Saying it opened her lungs and allowed her to breathe. She ran her hands over his arms, his shoulders, soaking him in.

He shook her off. "It won't work, Anna."

"It won't work the way it was," she told him. "It won't work with the old Anna." She couldn't believe she was saying this. These words, dumb and ridiculous sounding, were coming out of her mouth and they were true. "But this is the new Anna."

"Don't be melodramatic."

"I can't help it!" she told him. "You're walking away from me. You're leaving me and I can't stand it. I can't stand who I am and what I've become. I want to be the person I was with you. I want…"

He was silent and the silence was killing her. Her confidence began to leak out. The momentum and desperation of charging barefoot over city sidewalks toward the man she loved, ground to a halt.

She took a deep breath. Then another and it shuddered in her chest. The tears she never cried pooled in her eyes, ran down her cheeks. For the first time in her life, Anna wished that she was someone else entirely. Someone who knew the right words. Someone who wasn't turning into her mother and driving Sam away.

But then, she had just walked out of what should have been the biggest moment of her life. She wasn't sure, but she might have told Camilla to go ahead and fire her.

Her. Anna. She did that.

She had done things that, a few months ago, she would

have thought impossible. But she was a woman with a life now. And this man was a huge part of it.

She took a deep breath and felt something new fill her. Something strong and calm and confident. Something like what she felt for her sister, but bigger. Something like what she felt for Camilla but a million times stronger. She was still crying, somehow unable to stop, but she smiled so hard her face hurt.

"I love you," she breathed and Sam jerked as if he had been hit. "I know it's crazy, I don't know you very well and it's really kind of selfish, but I do. I love you and it's great to be able to say that."

"Anna..." Sam started to say and she put up her hand to stop him, words gurgling up in her from some unseen spring.

"You feel free to keep being mad. You deserve it, I was an ass. But I—" she shook her head the smile turning into a laugh "—love you and I am willing to do whatever it takes to make you feel the same way." She cupped his face in her hands and he didn't back away. "Because really, Sam, this, what I am feeling, what's happening to me right now, feels great. Feels like I am on fire or something. I'm flying."

He smiled briefly and she saw the war that was going on in him. Her nose was running and she swiped at it with the back of her hand.

"What about Arsenal?" he asked.

"I think I'm fired," she told him and she laughed. She couldn't believe it, but she sputtered and giggled and had to brace herself on Sam to keep from falling over. "Camilla looked pretty pissed."

"She still does," Sam whispered, his eyes lifted from her face to a place behind her. Anna turned.

Camilla was standing a few feet up the hill from them, an angry woman in silk and heels. "Camilla, you were right," she told her boss. "I work too hard." For the first time, she believed it and saw all the ugly things it was doing in her life. She shrugged feeling the weight of the world lift right off her back. "I quit."

"That might be a bit rash," Sam muttered from behind her.

"You quit?" Camilla repeated, her eyes narrowed. Now, she looked angry and shrewd. Anna nodded defenselessly.

"I can't keep going like this. I'm driving away the most important person in my life."

Marie came up behind Camilla and she put an arm around the older woman's waist. Anna's throat closed at the sight of them. From behind her Sam's hand, warm and heavy settled on her shoulder. His lips pressed against her hair and Anna felt it all the way in her heart.

She closed her eyes in ecstatic relief.

"See," Marie said to Camilla. "I told you, you just had to fight dirty and she'd come around."

Anna's eyes popped open and Sam's other hand came up to her shoulder. Holding her back.

"You were right." Camilla wrapped her arm around Marie's waist and they beamed at Anna. "Getting Aurora involved was her idea," Camilla told Anna as she pointed at Marie. "It was brilliant," she complimented Marie.

"Thank you. But really, the thing with Andrew…genius."

Camilla gave a little bow. "Calling Sam tonight. Truly the coup de grace."

"I was inspired."

The two continued to compliment each other and Anna breathed deep, calming breaths against the urge to kill. They knew. These two women. Her family. They set her up. All the dreams, the ulcers, the sleepless nights. The five thousand cups of chamomile tea with Aurora.

"All of this…?" Anna sputtered.

"Well, we wouldn't have had to if you had just taken a break like you were supposed to." Camilla scolded her. "Really, a fake boyfriend? What is this, a romance novel?"

"I'm afraid the second you told me your plan, I had to tell Camilla." Marie shrugged as though the whole thing had been beyond her control. Her big, fat mouth had never been something she could rein in.

"Did you know?" Anna asked Sam, wondering how much of this was real and hating the idea that any part of her life with Sam might have been insincere.

"I had no idea." He appeared a little shell-shocked. "They...?" He looked at Anna and she could only shrug. "Wow." He breathed. Anna smiled and looked down at her bare feet on the cement and wondered what to do now. How exactly did one fight for one's man when he didn't seem particularly keen on being fought for?

"You don't have to quit," Sam murmured in her ear and Anna looked deep into his green eyes so she wouldn't get this wrong. "You don't." He smiled at her. "You just have to slow down."

"Oh, I'm at a complete stop, Sam. I may never start again. In fact..." She turned back to Marie and Camilla. "I'm leaving ladies," she called out. "I've got five months of sabbatical."

"Three," Camilla pointed out.

"Not with the two months of work I just did. I'll see you in March." Before Camilla could protest she grabbed Sam by the hand and started down the hill. To where, she had no idea, but this was the direction Sam had been headed and she was going with him.

"Most important person in your life, huh?" he asked, pulling her up against his side. Her whole body woke up at the contact.

Well, hello again, her body hummed.

She stopped and pulled Sam into her arms. "I'll spend..." She swallowed completely sure of what she was saying, but not entirely confident in the strength of the limb under her feet. "The rest of my life proving that to you."

"Whoa!" His eyes opened wide, but he was laughing and she realized the limb was very strong indeed. "That's pretty fast for a woman I barely know."

"Well, you've got five months to fall in love."

She smiled, his arms sliding around her back. "I already have," he whispered just before his lips settled onto hers.

Come to Mama! Her body sang and her heart celebrated and Anna melted right into Sam.

Anna Simmons, she thought. *Top of the world.*

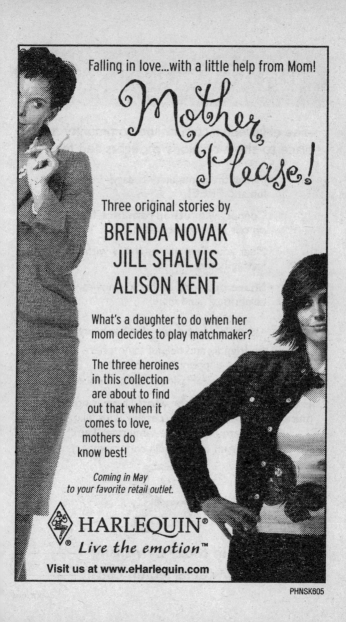

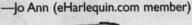

**A brand-new story from the *USA TODAY*
bestselling series, The Fortunes of Texas!**

SHOTGUN *Vows*

by award-winning author

TERESA SOUTHWICK

After one night of indulgent passion leaves Dawson Prescott and
Matilda Fortune trembling—and married!—they must decide if
their shotgun vows have the promise of true love.

Look for *Shotgun Vows* in May 2004.

The Fortunes of Texas:
Membership in this family has its privileges...and its price.
But what a fortune can't buy, a true-bred Texas love is sure to bring!

Where love comes alive™

Visit Silhouette at www.eHarlequin.com PSSV

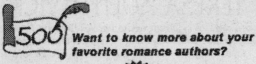

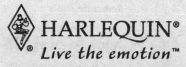

**Experience two super-sexy tales
from national bestselling author**

**A collector's size volume
of HOT summer reading!**

Two extraordinary women explore their deepest romantic desires
in Mallory's famously sensual novels, *Love Game* and *Love Play*.

Catch the sizzle…in May 2004!

"Ms. Rush provides an intense and outrageously sexy tale..."
—*Romantic Times*

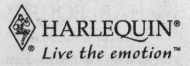

HARLEQUIN®
Live the emotion™

Visit us at www.eHarlequin.com

PHMR635